SECRET OF THE MISSING TENANT

SECRET OF THE MISSING TENANT

ADITYA BANERJEE

Srishti
Publishers & Distributors

Srishti Publishers & Distributors
A unit of AJR Publishing LLP
212A, Peacock Lane
Shahpur Jat, New Delhi – 110 049

editorial@srishtipublishers.com

First Published by Srishti Publishers & Distributors in 2025

10 9 8 7 6 5 4 3 2 1

This is a work of fiction. The characters, places, organisations and events described in this book are either a work of the author's imagination or have been used fictitiously. Any resemblance to people, living or dead, places, events, communities or organisations is purely coincidental.

Printed and bound in India.

For all those who have yet to
find their way home.

Abacus

Shankar stared at the stack of library books he planned to borrow, but his mind was elsewhere. *Why did the raids fail? They couldn't have known we were coming. We'd been staking out those warehouses for weeks. Is it possible they've infiltrated our police station?*

As the questions swirled in his head, movement registered in the corner of his eye. The head librarian and his new assistant were stealing glances at him, whispering among themselves.

Shankar pretended not to notice, gazing listlessly at the copy of the *Indian Gazette* on his desk. It was open to a black-and-white photo of the police academy and an article on the new recruits joining the Indian Police Service.

Nearly a decade had passed since Shankar, now in his thirties, had graduated from the academy. His time in the service had been checkered. While his current posting had brought him accolades—recent setbacks notwithstanding—his earlier tenure had been marred with accusations of heavy-handedness, not to mention the inquiry that left a stain on his permanent record.

After leafing through the pages, he glanced at his watch and sighed. It was time to head back to the station. Hauling himself to his feet, he picked up the stack of books, again noticing the old librarian and his assistant conspiring in hushed tones. Their wide eyes were fixed on him as they exchanged whispers. *What's this all about?*

Shankar, a frequent visitor to the library, had seen the old librarian a few times before. He marched toward the counter. The librarian gave him a sheepish smile when he placed his books on the large table with a thud.

"It's nice to see you again, Officer Sen," he murmured.

"Likewise. How are you today, Bharat Ji?" Shankar kept his tone cheerful.

Bharat motioned his assistant closer. "This is Hritesh. He joined a few weeks ago."

"Happy to see you've found some help," Shankar said, gently pushing the pile of books forward and reaching into his pocket for his library card.

"W-we were wondering," Bharat stuttered, looking at Hritesh anxiously.

"What is it, Bharat Ji? Is there something I can help you with?" Shankar asked as he clutched his card. He studied Bharat and then Hritesh, who started shuffling his feet.

"I am not sure, sir, if it is indeed anything. Maybe it's just..." Bharat trailed off, his face ashen.

Shankar smiled. "How about you tell me what's on your mind? Don't worry. If it turns out to be nothing, it won't matter."

"We don't want to waste your time," Bharat mumbled.

"That's all right. As a policeman, I'm well aware that not all complaints lead to anything worthwhile," Shankar continued.

"It's not so much a complaint as a strange occurrence." Bharat glanced at Hritesh, who nodded in agreement.

"In the library?" Shankar prodded.

"Overdue books from Mr Nath," Hritesh blurted, his outburst startling Bharat and Shankar.

"Not just that," Bharat sighed. "But yes, what I first noticed was that his books were overdue, and he is never late."

"Overdue books are hardly a call for concern. I am sure that at some point, he will show up to pay the required fines," Shankar said, tapping his fingers on the counter as his patience wore thin.

"It is more than that. You see, Mr Nath is my tenant. I own two small apartments in a building not far from here. I live in one and have rented out the second. A librarian's salary is hardly enough to live on, even for a widower," Bharat continued.

Shankar recalled Bharat mentioning how he had inherited two one-bedroom apartments from his parents. After his only daughter got married and moved to Lucknow following his wife's death, he continued working at the library past retirement to keep himself busy.

"Is it an issue of rent?" Shankar asked. "I am sorry, Bharat Ji, but I can't help you. You would have to lodge a complaint with the proper authorities."

"No, no! Nothing of that sort, officer," the librarian babbled, taking Shankar by surprise. "Quite the opposite. Dinesh Nath has never missed a payment."

"Then?" Shankar pressed, leaning in closer.

"We haven't seen him for nearly a week now. And it's quite unlike him to not show up without notice. You see, he works as a night watchman at the library on the weekends. We have had to hire a temporary worker to cover his shifts," Bharat said.

He glanced at Hritesh, who was now scribbling the details of Shankar's books into a large register. The assistant nodded in agreement.

Shankar paused, thinking it over, "There could be a more straightforward explanation. Maybe he is sick or visiting relatives. Perhaps a family emergency?"

"It is possible." Bharat stroked his chin. "He is not sick or holed up in his apartment. Of that, I am sure. I knocked on his door and haven't seen any lights on for the past few days. He always tells me when he is leaving town. And he certainly would have let me know if he wasn't coming to work." A shadow fell over his face. "I am telling you, sir, there is something wrong."

"I am guessing he is not from Delhi?"

"No, sir. He is from Mussoorie," Bharat replied. "But he wouldn't have left without telling us, even in an emergency."

"Do you know where he works?"

"He's a security guard in a warehouse on the outskirts of Delhi. And as I mentioned, he also works in this building on the weekends," Bharat explained. "He is a conscientious employee, dedicated, always on time."

Shankar's skin prickled, the hairs on his arms rising, "A warehouse, you say? Where outside of Delhi?" Shankar asked, unable to control the surge in his volume.

"Near the Haryana border, around Gurgaon," Bharat responded.

Shankar furrowed his brow. Though Bharat reached for the library card in his hand, Shankar still clutched it tightly, his mind reeling. *The warehouses we raided were along the Delhi-Gurgaon border. Could there be a connection?* Either way, it was worth looking into.

"Would I have seen Dinesh at the library?" Shankar asked.

Bharat straightened his back. "I doubt it, sir. He usually comes in just before closing and leaves before the library opens." Bharat lowered his voice and added, "He told Hritesh that he was worried about something, and he wondered if he should go to the police with his predicament."

"Worried about what?" Shankar asked, placing the card on the counter. Bharat cast a glance at Hritesh, gesturing for him to elaborate.

Hritesh shuffled back to the counter. "Sir, he claimed he had uncovered something that might interest the police and the press."

"What?"

"Sorry?" Hritesh asked, puzzled.

"I mean, what did he uncover?" Shankar clarified.

"He never got around to telling us what it was. I am afraid the library was crowded that day, and we couldn't pause for a proper conversation. He wanted to tell me more, but we never got around to it," Hritesh paused, his eyes downcast.

Shankar stopped to study the large calendar on the opposite wall. It was January 15, 1985. Only a few days until *I travel to Dehradun to visit Vikram.* The thought of seeing his son made him momentarily forget everything else, a smile tugging at his lips. He quickly pushed the thought aside and turned back to Bharat and Hritesh. "So, you haven't seen him for a week. Do you know whether anyone has reported him missing?"

"That's why we wanted to talk to you," Bharat rumbled. "If indeed someone has filed a missing person's report, it would most likely be in your police station since our apartment building is nearby."

"Well, that's not always the case," Shankar said softly. "I am curious. You said he works in a warehouse. Didn't the managers drop by to look for him? I am guessing they have his home address."

"No one has stopped by," Bharat replied firmly. "I would have known if anyone had come looking for him."

"How? You're here in the library all day."

"True, but they would have at least left a note in his mailbox," Bharat added.

Shankar sighed. "I am not sure—"

"I am telling you, sir, something is wrong here," Bharat pleaded. "What else could it be?"

"Oh, a great many things, Bharat Ji. I appreciate your concern for your tenant. But there are simpler explanations. Maybe his employer has sent him away on business," Shankar said, not believing his own words. This could be much more sinister if the warehouse was genuinely being used for the nefarious activities they'd been tracking. But he didn't want to raise alarms with the librarian.

"But he is a security guard," Bharat contended. "Why send him away?"

"Maybe he was tasked with accompanying a shipment from the warehouse to another destination. Or perhaps he did leave for an emergency visit to Mussoorie, and he didn't have time to inform you," Shankar said quickly.

Bharat breathed a sigh of resignation. He looked at Hritesh, and they both shook their heads, clearly unconvinced. Hritesh eventually fell silent and finished noting down what titles Shankar was borrowing. After a short pause, Shankar picked up the stack of books.

Bharat tried again in a weak voice, "Well, maybe we would feel better if you came and took a look at his apartment."

Shankar offered an apologetic smile. "Bharat Ji, you know that I strictly can't do that unless someone is reported missing or there is suspicion of a crime or some complaint. But—"

"I understand, sir," Bharat cut in. "We just thought we'd bring it to your attention. Perhaps it truly is nothing. If you choose to look into this, however, someone may be able to help."

"Who's that?" Shankar asked.

"A few weeks ago, one of his friends from Bombay dropped by. It seems Dinesh worked at a hotel on Marine Drive when he lived there." Bharat pivoted to Hritesh, who slipped a folded sheet of paper on the counter. "This is the name of his friend and the hotel where he works," Bharat continued, pointing to the paper.

Shankar picked it up and took a quick look, "This gentleman, Chirag Seth, is his friend from Bombay?"

"Yes. At least, it seemed that way. Dinesh introduced us to Chirag, who was very cordial. From the little we saw, they seemed close," Bharat responded.

"I assume you've already tried calling Chirag."

"We did. He told us that he hasn't been in touch with Dinesh since they last met in Delhi, here at the library," Bharat affirmed. "And then ..."

Shankar narrowed his eyes, not missing how Bharat's pupils darted as he spoke. "Is there something else that you are not telling me? About Chirag?"

Bharat and Hritesh shared a wary glance. Then, Bharat spoke slowly, as if choosing his following words carefully.

"No, not about Chirag."

"Then?"

Bharat checked to make sure no one was listening. "Dinesh never told us explicitly, but he was terrified during his last visit to the library. He kept muttering about something he had seen in the library or the warehouse where he works. He wouldn't stop glancing over his shoulder," Bharat said.

Shankar's scalp prickled. *So, there is something. And it might be connected to the gang operating in the warehouses. Was Dinesh a gang member who bolted once he figured out the police were on to them?*

"What do you mean, terrified?" Shankar pried.

"It was almost as if he thought someone was following him."

Shankar hummed to himself, "And this was how many days before he went missing?"

"I never saw him after that, not in the library or our building."

"Right," Shankar mumbled. His eyes roved to the exit of the library. A few students were filing through the doors, ambling to the sprawling desks in the centre of the room. He turned back to Bharat and Hritesh. "All right, here's what I'll do. First, I'll check if someone has filed a missing person's report on your tenant, Mr Dinesh Nath. If that's the case, I will follow up with the officer in charge to see where things stand. But I doubt one has been filed because someone would have contacted you since you are his landlord. Please let me know if you hear anything from Mr Nath or folks trying to locate him. You know where to find me."

"Yes, sir," Bharat said with a relieved smile. "Thank you for looking into it."

"I can't make any promises, Bharat Ji. If no investigation is underway, there's not much else I can do. As you can imagine, we are swamped with crimes that have already been committed."

"I understand, Officer," Bharat said.

"I'll be back in a few days to return the books. If there's still no word on him, we'll decide what to do next," Shankar added.

"Of course," Bharat reluctantly replied. The old librarian clearly wasn't happy that Shankar wouldn't be immediately diving into the disappearance. But his hands were tied. Without a complaint or a first information report, there wasn't much he could do. However, if Dinesh worked in one of the warehouses that had been raided, then it was worth looking into.

"If he's not back in a few days, you can lodge an FIR at the station," Shankar said. "You don't have to be family to do that, and your concern about his whereabouts makes me believe you genuinely care."

"I do, sir. He is a good man. It's just that ... something is irking me about this whole situation. I can't put my finger on it."

"I understand. We'll talk more this weekend," Shankar said. With a smile, he nodded at Bharat and Hritesh before exiting the library and heading back to the police station, unease brewing in his gut.

***

When he returned to his charcoal-grey office at the station, Shankar couldn't help but note the contrast between the modern library, with its large windows spanning every wall, and the dimly lit police station. The building was a relic from colonial times. The facade resembled an old, refurbished manor, and the interior was spacious enough. But the flickering fluorescent lights and dark walls created a cold, damp atmosphere. After settling into his comfortable chair, he called for his constable, Ashok.

Rubbing his arms as a cool draft swept over him, he glanced at the far end of his large office, which held a bookcase, a small sofa, and a coffee table. The cramped window was firmly shuttered, and a noisy heater beneath it was trying to keep the room warm.

There was a knock on the door opposite the window. Shankar quickly waved Ashok inside, pointing to one of the four chairs across his desk. The constable, a tall man with a strong build, settled in, and they quickly reviewed the files waiting on his desk. With that finished, Shankar set down his pen and locked eyes with Ashok.

"Do you know the South Delhi Public Library, the one that I frequent?"

"Yes, sir," Ashok said with a curt nod. Shankar then relayed everything he had heard from the old librarian and his assistant earlier that day.

Shankar paused to let the information sink in. "What do you think?"

"Did he say which warehouse Dinesh works at?"

"No. It seems Dinesh never shared that with them."

"Strange. As a tenant, I'd have expected him to share his place of employment with his landlord," Ashok stated.

Shankar nodded, peering at his constable, "Tell me, what's your gut telling you?"

"At this point, it looks like nothing more than some overdue books and a tenant who left in a hurry, either for work or to visit his family," Ashok declared, leaning back in his chair. "But this warehouse connection. I mean, sir, what are the chances that—"

"That's precisely what doesn't sit right with me." Shankar gazed toward the window. *And the fact that the raids failed. And that we might have a mole in the station.* Was there a link between Dinesh and the failed raids? It didn't make sense.

"Something is bothering you, sir. It's more than just the connection to the warehouse, isn't it?"

"Well, yes," Shankar remarked, his eyes roving to the ceiling fan. "This Dinesh fellow was scared of something right before he disappeared. And then, there's ..." His gaze fell to the clock on the opposite wall.

"What is it, sir?" Ashok prodded.

"It's what they said about him," Shankar responded. "Everything they shared about Dinesh suggests that he is a creature of habit. He returns library books on time, is always punctual when coming to work, is never late when paying rent, and always informs his landlord before he leaves for any trips. A man of singular habits, it seems. Folks like that don't just bolt without telling anyone."

"Maybe there was an emergency—" Ashok started, but Shankar raised his arm slightly to stop him.

"Perhaps, but I need you to find out whether anyone has filed a missing person's report at our station and maybe the two other nearby stations."

"Right, sir," Ashok hunched forward to scribble something on his notepad.

"Also, I want you to visit the library tomorrow morning before coming in to work so you can get the address of Dinesh's family in Mussoorie. As his landlord, Bharat should have those details. We need his photograph as well."

Ashok nodded, "Anything else, sir?"

"Yes. Ask the old librarian and his assistant whether they have any more details about the warehouse where Dinesh works. They may not have the address, but maybe they know what goods the warehouse stored or the nature of Dinesh's security work there."

"If I locate his workplace, do you want me to go there, sir?"

"No," Shankar said, his voice firm. "Let's flesh out the details, and then we'll take it from there."

"Right." Ashok pushed out of his chair.

"Oh, and the friend who came from Bombay," Shankar amended, snapping his fingers. Ashok sat back down to jot down the details while Shankar went on. "Call him up, this Chirag Seth fellow. See if he can tell us anything."

"Yes, sir," Ashok said.

"I know I've given you a few errands, but this doesn't take priority over our other cases. Is that understood?"

He gave a quick nod.

"All right, off you go, then. We'll talk again about the narcotics investigation once we get more details from our colleagues in Rajasthan. That remains our top priority," Shankar reaffirmed.

Ashok nodded once more and left the room. Getting up, Shankar shuffled over to the window and opened it. He shut off the heater and gazed at the fleet of police Jeeps and vans congregating along the street and in the parking lot. Yet another raid was being planned, targeting various locations in the city following a lengthy investigation between Delhi Police and agencies in the neighbouring states.

Over the last few weeks, they'd managed to nab a few low-level gang operatives. Interrogating them had revealed several hideouts. Shankar and his team had conducted a few stakeouts and raids on the factories and warehouses, but the results had been disappointing. That investigation consumed most of Shankar's time—and the station's resources.

Shankar's superiors were under a lot of pressure, from both the public and the press, to stem the flow of illicit drugs and contraband being smuggled across the border into the western states and Delhi, which was quickly becoming the primary hub for dealers and consumers.

Shankar was pulled from his thoughts by the shrill ring of his phone. When he picked it up, he was summoned—along with his colleagues from other stations—to a meeting with officials in the Home Ministry regarding their ongoing investigation.

Over the next few days, Shankar and his team were once again swamped with activities related to the narcotics case. They investigated illicit activities and carried out raids on the outskirts of Delhi, all with limited success. It wasn't until Friday, when Ashok and Shankar were driving together, that they finally had a chance to discuss the old librarian's missing tenant.

"A bit of a dead end, sir." Ashok stared out the side window as he spoke. Shankar instructed his driver to drop Ashok off before heading to his residence.

"How so?" Shankar angled himself sideways in the back seat of the large Ambassador.

"I obtained the address of Dinesh Nath's parents in Mussoorie. I called them, but they hadn't heard from him in days. However, they mentioned that this wasn't abnormal. It seems Dinesh is estranged from his family."

Shankar wrinkled his forehead. "Estranged? Why?"

"He eloped with someone, and the family wasn't too happy with the union. They've been on bad terms ever since," Ashok revealed.

"How odd. Bharat and Hritesh never mentioned that Dinesh

was married," Shankar said, scratching his chin. "They made it sound like he was living alone."

"I can't say, sir. I only know that his family in Mussoorie is not concerned about his radio silence," Ashok stated.

"Did you speak to them directly?"

"No. I called the Mussoorie Police Station and asked a constable to look them up. He was the one who relayed all this to me. Dinesh's family doesn't have a phone at their residence."

"What about missing person's reports?" Shankar pressed.

"Nothing whatsoever in our station—or other nearby stations, for that matter. It seems no one besides the librarian is too bothered that he is missing." Ashok shrugged.

Shankar paused, listening to the hum of the engine. "Strange, isn't it?"

"I will tell you what is strange, sir."

"What's that?" Shankar turned back to his constable, wondering what else he missed.

"No one knows where he worked. I mean, aside from the library where he was a night watchman," Ashok said.

"So, this warehouse ..."

"No one seems to know anything about it," Ashok continued. "I pressed the librarian and his assistant, and they couldn't tell me a single detail. His family in Mussoorie were just as clueless. I am beginning to wonder if he even works there. Over the past few days, no one has contacted Bharat regarding Dinesh or come by his apartment to find out why he hasn't been showing up for work."

"Yet he pays his rent on time," Shankar remarked. "You think he has another source of income?"

Ashok raised his eyebrows. "You mean something illegal, sir?"

"Perhaps."

"I can't say. But I do think we should check out his apartment. Maybe that will reveal something. Right now, we are in the dark," Ashok concluded.

"Agreed." Shankar bobbed his head lightly.

After a moment, the driver pulled up outside Ashok's residence. Before the constable could get out, Shankar caught his gaze. "Let's visit Bharat at his home tomorrow morning. I assume you got his address."

"I did, sir." Ashok hesitated before turning the handle to open the door.

"Is there something you want to add? Something bothering you about Dinesh Nath?"

Ashok paused before responding. "Concerning Dinesh Nath, only that no one seems to be missing him, if you catch my meaning, sir. I wanted to say more about the raids we carried out earlier."

"Oh, what about them?" Shankar asked, surprised by the change of topic.

"They didn't yield much, did they? Our past raids have always produced better results, and we never failed to nab someone or even a few suspects. But these hideouts were sparsely manned, and we found so little," Ashok declared.

Shankar knew he was right. It was bothering him as well. "What are you suggesting, Ashok?"

"I can't say for sure, sir. But it would almost seem they knew we were coming," Ashok said, his voice low.

"That's quite a theory, but not all that far-fetched. For now, let's keep this to ourselves, shall we? We can discuss this further at the station tomorrow after visiting Bharat," Shankar suggested.

"Of course, sir. Have a good evening." With that, Ashok quickly departed.

On the ride home, Shankar mulled over Ashok's suspicions.

Shankar himself had long suspected a mole in their station. Then, there was Dinesh Nath. So many things failed to add up.

Once he turned in for the night, Shankar tossed and turned in bed. Eventually, he gave up and grabbed one of the books he had borrowed from the library, opening the cover to the first page. As he read, his eyes began to blur as he drifted off, and before he knew it, he woke up with a start. Sweat matted his hair to his forehead and dripped down his arms.

It was the same dream, so eerily familiar yet impossible to explain. He staggered over to his desk, pulled out a clean sheet of paper, and started writing it down from the perspective of someone on the outside looking in.

Shankar steps away from his car, his grey trousers pressed and new. A faint breeze ruffles his hair.

He seems to be walking toward a shop that looms ahead of him. As he nears the building, the merchandise gleams through the windows. It's an old watch shop. He pushes the door and steps inside.

Once there, Shankar is dazzled by the rustic interior. Clocks of all shapes and sizes line the walls and shelves—new clocks, antique clocks, grandfather clocks, wristwatches in glass cases, cuckoo clocks, and all sorts of alarm clocks.

A mechanical sound rings out from one of the timepieces behind him. Shankar turns slowly, gravitating toward it.

On the other side of the counter, a man stands with his back to Shankar. When Shankar unhooks his wristwatch and places it on the glass countertop, the storekeeper turns to face him.

Do I know him? He looks familiar.

The man opens his mouth to speak. "How can I help you, sir?"

"My watch has stopped. I need to get it fixed," Shankar replies, pointing to the watch.

"Just a moment, sir." The storekeeper peers at the watch and

smiles. "Got stuck at 12 a.m. or p.m., do you remember?"

"I don't. I mean ... I-I can't recall when it happened," Shankar stutters.

"Let me fix this for you. Meanwhile, care to look at a few new models?"

"I am not sure." Shankar hesitates, then shrugs.

The storekeeper places two boxes of wristwatches in front of him. As Shankar starts looking them over, the man works on his watch.

Strangely enough, every watch Shankar picks up has stopped at twelve sharp.

"Excuse me. What's wrong with these watches? They are all stuck at the same time," Shankar stammers, rattled by confusion.

The storekeeper returns to the counter, examines them, and then locks eyes with Shankar. "They are not stuck at the same time, sir. It's you that's probably stuck."

"What do you mean?"

"You know precisely what I mean," the storekeeper says, handing a watch to Shankar.

Shankar squints, scrutinising the man. "You look familiar."

"I am sure I do," the storekeeper replies with a smile.

Shankar glances around at the empty store, gazing past the large glass windows facing the street. He can't spot a single soul.

"Why are the streets empty?"

The storekeeper smiles. "You still don't understand, do you, sir?"

Shankar continues to stare through the shop window. No, he cannot understand. He turns back to the new watches. This time, each one is running perfectly. He grabs one, and the second hand goes still.

"These watches stop when I touch them. What's going on?" Shankar demands.

"What do you think, sir?" The shopkeeper stares back with a

knowing glint in his eye.

"Am I dead? Or am I just alone?" Shankar asks, looking around before finally fixing his gaze on the storekeeper. He looks so familiar. Is Shankar looking at himself? An older version of him? Before he can utter a question, the man responds.

"No, sir. I am dead. But you're alone."

Shankar's confusion melts away, and his eyes widen. He can now see through the veil, and he recognises the storekeeper.

"But it's time for you to figure out who killed me. Time for you to wake up."

Shankar's vision begins to fade, and all the clocks in the store chime at once. The deafening roar wakes him with a start.

Shankar reread the detailed scene he just wrote down, gulping down a glass of water. The dream, the conversation with the man, and all the clocks in the store were always so clear. But he couldn't quite place the store or the shopkeeper. *Why am I having the same dream over and over again? And what could it mean?* He stole a glance at the small clock on his desk and sighed. It was time to get some sleep—hopefully, without any more dreams.

***

When Shankar and Ashok arrived at Bharat's building the following day, they looked around before knocking at the librarian's apartment. The building was one of many mid-rises perched on a busy intersection in the heart of Delhi. The structure was in want of some repair. Paint peeled off the sides, and a narrow, unkempt garden with long grasses and tangling vines surrounded it. Unlocked wooden gates marked the two entrances, and Shankar could make out eyes peering at them from a few balconies of the four-story structure. There was no elevator, so they took the stairs. Once they reached the second story, where Bharat's apartment was located, Shankar was surprised when the door flew open without them even knocking.

"Good morning, sir," Bharat said to Shankar, then nodded to Ashok. "I saw you arriving from my balcony."

"Good morning, Bharat Ji. This is Ashok, my trusted aide whom you have already met. We were on our way to the station and decided to drop by. Have you heard from Dinesh?" Shankar asked.

Before answering, Bharat motioned them through the doorway, leading them into the small living room. He pointed to a sofa next to a window, where Shankar and Ashok made themselves comfortable. The door to the other room was open, and Shankar stole a quick peek at the sparsely furnished bedroom. A small kitchenette and a bathroom on opposite sides of the living room summed up the entire place.

"No, I haven't heard from Dinesh," Bharat said as he sat on one of the wooden chairs across the sofa. "Would you like some tea?"

"Oh, no," Shankar said quickly, noticing that Ashok was about to respond differently. "We're in a bit of a hurry."

"I am guessing, sir, that you were unable to determine Dinesh's whereabouts," Bharat said, leaning forward.

"That's why we wanted to stop by. Would it be possible for us to see his apartment? I am assuming you have a spare key."

His eyes flitted nervously. "I do, sir. I'd be glad to help. But I don't want to get into any trouble. When he returns and learns that I let you in, he may not be thrilled."

"I will take full responsibility, Bharat Ji. Don't worry. If it comes to that, you can blame it all on me. In any case, we're not conducting a search. We are just looking for something that might help us locate him. I promise we won't make a mess," Shankar said with a smirk.

"I am sure you won't, sir," Bharat responded, straightening his back to get up. Shankar raised his palm, gesturing for him to wait.

"Before that, we were hoping you could help us with something else," Shankar added.

"Sure. How can I help?" Bharat reclined in his chair.

"Do you know whether Dinesh is married?" Judging by Bharat's wide-eyed reaction, the question took him by surprise.

"Not as far as I know. He keeps mostly to himself, but I'd know if he were married. He rarely has friends over, and I don't recall any woman staying with him," Bharat said, his voice soft.

"Did you ever ask him outright?" Shankar pressed.

"I did. Once. This was when he first rented the apartment a few months ago," Bharat replied, stroking his chin.

"And?" Shankar shuffled his feet.

"Now that you mention it, he never categorically stated that he was single. He was rather coy, and he seemed to suggest there was someone in his hometown. When I asked, he got rather agitated and quickly changed the subject. I didn't bring it up again. Our conversations always centred on current events, cricket, and politics. We rarely talked about his family or our pasts." Bharat paused, gazing off to the side at a wall clock before returning to Shankar. "Is he married, sir?"

"We don't know everything just yet," Shankar asserted. "But there's one more thing."

"Yes?"

"Ashok mentioned that you haven't a clue where this warehouse is, the one where Dinesh works." Shankar cast a glance at Ashok.

"Unfortunately, I don't," Bharat replied, shaking his head.

"I understand. But is there anything that he may have told you in passing that could help us find this warehouse?"

"I don't know, sir. He mentioned once that it was a storage facility where some electrical components were assembled and packed in large containers. I am afraid that's all I can recall," Bharat answered thoughtfully.

"That's all right. Now, let's look at Dinesh's apartment, shall we?" Shankar slowly got up, and Ashok followed suit. Bharat guided them out of the apartment and into a corridor. Four apartments occupied each floor, and Dinesh's was across from Bharat's. The elderly librarian brought out a set of keys and shuffled through them before carefully unlocking the door. He was about to enter the doorway when Shankar touched his arm and gestured for him to wait outside.

Ashok was the first to enter, and Shankar trailed close behind. The apartment's layout was identical to Bharat's but even more sparsely furnished. The living room comprised a small dining table, four chairs, and a sofa set. A compact desk was wedged against the wall, and a nearby bookcase was stuffed with various books. The desk lamp was still on. The kitchenette looked clean, as though it had rarely been used. Ashok took his time surveying the room while Shankar crept into the bedroom.

A large bed propped against the wall occupied most of the floor space. Against the opposite wall, yet another small bookcase was crammed with books, papers, and fliers. A small walk-in closet held the man's clothes, all neatly arranged. Under the bed were two suitcases that stored more clothes. Slowly and thoroughly, Shankar rifled through the contents of the closet, the suitcases, and the bookcase. Shankar gestured toward the living room when Ashok walked in to check on him.

"Go through the contents of the other bookcase and check

for any mail or other papers. Let's see if we can locate the address of Dinesh's employer."

"Yes, sir." Ashok marched out of the room, and Shankar returned to his task.

After half an hour, Shankar and Ashok switched rooms. They then looked over the kitchen, the bathroom, and the small balcony. Once they finished their sweep, they sat down at the dining table. While glancing around the room for anything they missed, Shankar noticed an envelope in Ashok's hand. It was Ashok who finally broke the silence.

"This is a strange apartment, wouldn't you say, sir?"

"How so?" Shankar asked, wondering what Ashok may have inferred from scrutinising the rooms.

"For one, I have never seen an apartment so tidy. It almost looks like a hotel room. The dust is expected since no one's been here for a few days. But nothing—I mean absolutely nothing—seems out of place," Ashok said, his brow wrinkled.

"What else?" Shankar asked with a secretive smile, watching his constable. He wondered whether Ashok had picked up on the one thing that did seem out of place compared to everything else in the apartment.

Ashok touched his chin in thought. "He seems to receive hardly any mail."

"That's right." Shankar nodded, peering at the bookcase and then toward the bedroom. "Tell me, Ashok. You are still single, right?"

"Yes, sir," Ashok replied with a puzzled look.

"And your quarters must be bigger than this, more spacious," Shankar continued.

"My apartment has two bedrooms. And yes, sir, it is quite a bit larger."

"And you have pictures of your parents, siblings, and friends..."

"Yes! That's what's weird about this place. There are no photographs anywhere," Ashok blurted, slamming his hand on the table.

"But it's not only that," Shankar mused, glancing at the window and then again toward the bedroom.

"What else, sir?"

"All the clothes are neatly arranged, tucked away in the closet. Now, wouldn't you expect some of the shelves and hangers to be empty if you were to go somewhere? And where is the dirty linen? Plus, his table lamp was still on."

"You're right, sir. Even the suitcases below the bed are organised. Plus, his toothbrush and shaving kit are still in the bathroom. It doesn't look like Dinesh left town," Ashok concluded.

Shankar nodded in agreement, his mind reeling with questions. He pointed to the envelope that Ashok was still clutching. "What's that you found?"

"A bank statement, sir, with the address of the bank. I was wondering if we might contact them for details regarding his employer and to discover if Dinesh has a proper job. The bank would know who is depositing money into the account. But..." Ashok opened the folded paper in the envelope and glared at it.

"But what?"

"This statement only shows cash deposits and withdrawals."

Shankar cocked his head to the side. "What do you mean? Even if he isn't truly employed at this mysterious warehouse, he is a library employee, and those deposits must be listed in the statement," he asserted, pointing to the paper.

"They aren't here, sir," Ashok mumbled. "Maybe he has another account?"

"That's possible," Shankar said. "Did you find anything to indicate that he's married?"

Ashok nodded, pointing to the bookcase. "It's easy to miss, but one of the books on the lowest shelf has a note on the inner cover. It's a gift from a friend in Jaisalmer, addressed to Mr and Mrs Nath. I can't imagine the book was a gift to his parents. Dinesh must be married."

"Right. Good find, Ashok. I almost missed it myself," Shankar said with a sly smile.

"But I did miss something. Didn't I, sir?"

"Well, don't beat yourself up. It isn't exactly something you'd recognise unless you knew what it was," Shankar said. He got up from his chair, walked over to the bookcase, and retrieved a small wooden box from the top shelf. He removed the item and placed it on the dining table. "Do you know what this is?"

Ashok studied it carefully. "I've seen it in gift shops, sir, but I assumed it was some decorative item. I've also seen it on desks at fancy hotels, fireplace mantels, and high-end stores. Honestly, I don't know what it could be."

"It's an abacus," Shankar said, bringing it closer to Ashok. "Now, this is an expensive one, excellent quality. Something that you won't find easily in stores. You may have seen simpler versions of it in toy shops."

"Yes! Now I remember," Ashok boomed. "Most of the ones I've seen have multi-coloured balls."

"Correct." Shankar nodded and continued, "If you look inside the box, there's something else." Shankar reached in and brought out a long, embroidered muslin cloth.

"Yes, I thought this was used to clean this contraption—I mean, abacus," Ashok said.

"No, it's a dupatta. I am guessing this was a gift." He examined the scarf-like cloth, the kind women wore over their heads. This one was relatively small. "Did you look at the toothbrushes in the cabinet behind the bathroom mirror?"

"Yes, there were a few extra brushes," Ashok responded.

"True, but did you check their sizes?"

"No, sir," Ashok mumbled.

"If you look carefully, you will notice that one belongs to a child."

"A child?" Ashok nearly shouted.

"Yes. There is something strange going on here. I bet if you checked with the bank, they would have no knowledge of his employer. And you are right. This apartment looks like a hotel room rather than a home. To top it off, Dinesh is indeed married, but he didn't share that with Bharat," Shankar listed off.

"And the abacus and dupatta?" Ashok asked, pointing to the box's contents on the table.

"That suggests a little girl was in this apartment at some point. We don't know who she is, but Dinesh also seems to have hidden her existence," Shankar uttered.

Change

Nitya glanced back as she rushed to the conference room for the morning meeting. Swati was having a hard time keeping up. Her younger assistant despised these sessions as much as she did, but they had no choice. *The Daily Citizen News,* a large, established paper, had acquired the smaller newspaper that employed them. The buyout had been fraught with misconduct accusations, office politics, and managers jostling for power and visibility.

Luckily, the new management had retained Nitya and half of her previous team. A buyout always brought uncertainty, and although the initial round of layoffs had ended, the remaining staff were unsure about what lay ahead. Was this a deliberate ploy by the executive team to keep them on their toes? At times like these, Nitya longed for her days at *The Callipur Times*, the small regional paper in her hometown where she'd started her career.

In *The Daily Citizen News*, she was just one of many senior managers, and it was easy to get lost in the crowd. What she objected to most was the paper's vision. Selling sensationalism was prioritised, with good investigative journalism falling by the wayside.

Once they entered the conference room, Nitya and Swati were inundated with back-to-back presentations on increasing readership and reducing overhead.

After two gruelling hours, Nitya emerged from the room and instructed Swati to join her at a nearby café. It was one of many that had sprung up in Connaught Place to cater to the young workforce whose employers boasted offices in the area. The silver lining of the whole ordeal was working in this posh neighbourhood of New Delhi. As they settled into their café booth, Nitya noticed some of their new colleagues enjoying the bright winter sun on the pavement outside. Once they ordered tea and a round of samosas, they launched into their unfinished conversation from the night before.

"This acquisition has been a nightmare. What a lousy meeting, ma'am," Swati grumbled. She glanced around, ensuring they were out of earshot of their colleagues.

"I don't know. It's certainly a different organisation in terms of culture and vision," Nitya contended. Swati wrung her hands and leaned closer.

"I'm just not sure we fit in. I understand the paper's a business, and increasing subscriptions and circulation pay our salaries. Still, there was no talk of improving the content, let alone addressing the issues that have arisen due to the acquisition," Swati said in a low voice.

"You have a point, but it's only been a few weeks. I am sure things will improve with time." Nitya folded her hands on the table, feeling more unsure than she let on.

"It's only gotten worse since we joined their workforce. I can't imagine things improving with the current leadership team," Swati sighed.

Nitya kept silent. She knew that her young assistant was right. She harboured the same concerns, and in her meetings with the new management team, she'd grown convinced that *The Daily Citizen News* was a different kettle of fish. After a few minutes, the samosas and tea arrived, interrupting her thoughts. Nitya felt better when she started eating. Swati, clearly hungry, wolfed down her food quickly before sipping the ginger tea she had ordered.

"Look, Swati. I know things are shaky; perhaps it will take time to improve. We have to prove ourselves with our hard work."

"I'm not sure this paper values that," Swati mumbled.

"What makes you say that?"

"I heard through the grapevine that the people being promoted are the ones close to the owners or those who publish sensational stories and scandals. The more mud you sling, the higher up you go," Swati stated, taking another sip.

"I think that's a bit of an exaggeration," Nitya said with a hint of a smile, wondering if the office gossip was feeding into some of this frenzy.

"Well, you heard about the evening edition they're planning. It's essentially a tabloid," Swati said. "*The Evening Spice*. Can you imagine? The name says it all." She shook her head.

"I have heard about that, but that's a different organisation," Nitya said, furrowing her brow.

"No, ma'am. They'll be feeding us stories with photos of politicians and celebrities, hoping the general public laps them up. As one of the managers put it, if there isn't a controversy, they would create one."

"Wow, that is quite a stretch. I wasn't aware of that angle," Nitya mumbled, taken aback.

"Well, now you know, ma'am."

"It helps to have a clever assistant manager on my team," Nitya added with a smile. Swati averted her gaze, her expression still troubled. "Look," Nitya continued, "I know you're worried. We all are. Everyone's jostling for visibility right now. But the only thing we can do is focus on our jobs and present the stories, ensuring the company understands what we bring to the table."

"That's what I'm worried about. I don't think they will, and.. She trailed off, her gaze darting.

"And what?" Nitya pressed.

"Ma'am, I need this job. I am getting married in a few months. Sure, my fiancé isn't exactly thrilled about me working here after what I told him about the new vision. But we both need to work and ..." Swati's voice faltered.

"I understand," Nitya said. "You are one of my best journalists, and I will do everything possible to keep the rest of my team intact. I certainly don't want to lose you."

"I know that, ma'am. What worries me is that it may not be in your control."

Nitya stared at her tea. "I know. I can't speak for anyone else, especially if the decision is made without my knowledge or input," Nitya responded, to which Swati nodded slowly. Nitya drew a sharp breath. "Well then, shall we talk about work?"

"Sure, ma'am," Swati responded in a more upbeat tone, straightening her back.

"Where are we with the narcotics story?" Nitya asked.

"We've managed to get statements from the police, but they didn't divulge much, claiming that it's an active investigation," Swati replied. She reached into her bag, brought out a notepad, and started reading her notes. "We also have a name from one of our contacts. Someone who was involved in a related case."

"What does that mean?"

"That this person may be able to assist us in identifying the route the smugglers take when hauling drugs across the border," Swati said, her eyes scanning her notepad.

"And how does this person have that intel? Was he part of a different gang? I mean, this all sounds rather suspicious, doesn't it?"

"Well, we know him in a sense. We interviewed him on another story we ran a few months back about the hideouts the smugglers have been using to store their cache," Swati continued.

"I remember that. The story came about rather by accident, didn't it? The police had conducted a raid and then called the press to show off what they had confiscated," Nitya said.

"Yes, the same, ma'am. If you recall, we pursued a follow-up story to uncover whether there was a bigger conspiracy involving these warehouse owners and drug smugglers. This gentleman had given us a short interview—off the record, of course. But he was rather coy in giving out details," Swati stated.

Nitya hummed in thought. "And now he wants to help us. Why?"

"I don't think he wants to, but the havildar at the police station mentioned that this fellow may have more details if we dig further," Swati responded. She glanced around and gestured to the waiter to bring her more tea. Nitya asked for another cup as well.

"So, what's the fellow's name? Where does he work?"

"Well, our contact at the station couldn't give us the warehouse details, or maybe he didn't want to. But this havildar did say that the man, Dinesh Nath, works at the South Delhi Public Library as a night watchman on weekends," Swati continued, referring to her notes.

"Perhaps we could visit him just before the library closes tomorrow."

"That's what I am planning," Swati offered.

"I'll join you. I need to get some books anyway. I hardly read nowadays—not counting what we must read as part of our job." Nitya sighed. "What else?"

"There's also the recent raids that the police conducted simultaneously throughout the city," Swati added quickly, pausing as the waiter cleared their table and placed a fresh teapot with two new cups before them. After thanking him, Swati continued, "The police are less enthusiastic about talking about their most recent raids. That's the way it seems to me, anyway."

"Why do you think that is?" Nitya asked. She poured some tea for Swati and herself, careful not to spill a drop on the table.

"I am not sure. I probed the folks at the station, but no one seemed willing to talk. The feeling I got was that the raids didn't result in a big catch of drugs. At least, that's what I could gather," Swati mused.

"Well, that tells me there's more to the story than they let on. Let's keep digging, contact some of our other sources, and see if we get anywhere," Nitya said before sipping ginger tea, its warming spices coating her tongue.

Swati nodded. "There's another thing, ma'am."

"What is it?"

"Our colleagues in the Jaipur office are hearing whispers of raids at the border near Jaisalmer. They are not sure whether they're related to drugs or arms. But it seems likely. What are the odds that they are not connected in some way?"

"True. Well, if they are, we might have another story," Nitya said with a smile.

Swati scrunched her eyebrows. "What story is that?"

"That the police and the security agencies have a leaky ship. If my assistant knows about the impending raids, I am sure the gang knows about them too," Nitya replied.

"So, you think there is a mole or informant in the police?"

"It wouldn't be too far-fetched to assume that someone, or maybe a few people, in each station are on the gang's payroll. They could be keeping them apprised of what's happening," Nitya contended.

"True," Swati murmured with a slight nod.

"Well, it's time to head back to the office. There's a lot to be done. Good work, by the way." Nitya cast her assistant a grateful smile before calling for the bill.

"Yes, and thank you, ma'am." Swati sighed, closing her notepad and slipping it back into her bag.

***

The drive to the South Delhi Public Library didn't take long. Nitya had asked Swati to meet her there. In the meantime, she enjoyed wandering around the cosy building nestled in a leafy neighbourhood of New Delhi. The new two-story library was a crowning jewel of the locality. The ground floor held tall cases of reference books, newspapers, and magazines along the walls, and the centre housed a collection of desks for patrons who wanted to spend time reading or studying. The second floor was a long mezzanine with high ceilings visible from the ground floor. There, the library boasted an extensive collection of books in multiple languages. Nitya noted that the building wasn't crowded, and a few students were already trickling out. She checked her watch. There was still half an hour before it was due to close.

"Strange," Nitya said, turning to her young assistant.

"What's that, ma'am?"

"I'd have never guessed so many people used the section for reference books," Nitya continued, pointing to an aisle on the opposite side.

"Why not?"

"I don't know. Anyhow, let's focus on the task at hand."

"Sure," Swati murmured, pointing to the large mahogany counter.

A few staff were poring over their open registers, busy tallying and sorting books. Nitya approached an elderly gentleman who stood behind the nearest desk.

"Excuse me, sir. Where can we find Mr Dinesh Nath?"

The man looked up with a start. "I am sorry, but who are you?" Nitya didn't miss the surprise in his voice as he hauled himself up from behind his desk. He shuffled up to Nitya and Swati, the ample counter standing between them.

"My name is Nitya Chaturvedi, and this is Swati Mullick. We're reporters from *The Daily Citizen News* and were told we could meet Mr Nath at the library. I believe he works as a night guard. Is our understanding correct?"

Nitya studied the old man, who seemed lost in thought. His eyes flitted around the room, his brow furrowing. "Who told you that you could find him here?"

"One of our contacts," Nitya responded, keeping things deliberately vague. She wasn't sure whether the old librarian would be forthcoming if they told him it was someone at the police station.

A shadow fell over his eyes. "Nitya Ji, we haven't heard from Dinesh Nath for over a week. We have contacted the police, and they are currently making inquiries."

"Oh!" Nitya gasped, pivoting to Swati, who looked equally surprised. "Have the police been able to locate him?"

"No," the old man said, his voice gruff. "They questioned me and my assistant and went through his apartment, but they haven't told us anything since then."

"What do you mean, went through his apartment?" Nitya asked.

"He lives in the same building as me, and I am his landlord," the man responded. A beat passed before he continued. "Unfortunately, I don't know anything more. If you need more details, please get in touch with the police station in Jorbagh."

"Understood," Nitya said. "You are ..."

"Bharat. I am the head librarian here," the old man stated, his voice firm.

"Bharat Ji, you have been of immense help already. We have a couple more questions, and if you cannot answer or choose not to, we completely understand," Nitya spoke slowly, trying not to frighten him off.

"Please, ask away. If it helps in locating Dinesh, I am happy to help. Hopefully, unlike the police, you will tell me how your search is going," Bharat grumbled.

"We will," Nitya affirmed.

"Well, then. What else do you want to know?"

"From our contact, we understand that Dinesh works in a warehouse. Do you know where it might be located?"

"No. He never told me the name of the company he worked for during the week nor the warehouse address," Bharat responded.

"Hmm," Nitya mumbled. She noticed Swati fidgeting from the corner of her eye as if itching to add something. She gestured for her to join the conversation.

"Bharat Ji, our contact, mentioned he has been working here for a few months. Where was he working before that?" she asked, whipping out her notepad.

Bharat fell silent, looking reflective. When he snapped out of his reverie, he called out for his assistant. A lanky man in his mid-twenties ambled sheepishly toward the counter, and Bharat met him halfway. Nitya strained her ears to hear as Bharat and the young man whispered among themselves. Then, they strode up to where Nitya and Swati waited. "This is my assistant, Hritesh. He is closer to Dinesh than I am and may be of greater assistance."

Hritesh nodded, stepping forward to speak. "Dinesh Ji is

originally from Mussoorie, but before coming to Delhi, he worked in Bombay for a few years."

"Did he say where?" Swati asked.

Nitya stood back, deciding to let her drive the conversation.

"Yes. He was employed at a showroom in Andheri that sold air coolers, and before that, he worked at a hotel on Marine Drive," Hritesh said before adding, "I don't know the name of the showroom, but a friend from the hotel came by a few weeks ago to meet him. I have his name and the hotel's address. Please give me a minute, and I will note it down for you."

With that, Hritesh disappeared into a small room behind the main counter. He quickly reappeared with a paper that he handed to Swati. "Before you ask, we have already contacted Chirag Seth. He said he hasn't heard from Dinesh in a while."

"Thank you for this," Swati said, carefully tucking the paper into her purse. After glancing at the pictures on the wall near the large clock, she turned to Hritesh. "This may sound odd, but bear with me. It may help us figure out where Mr Nath is," Swati started cautiously. "Do you happen to have his photograph?"

"We do. We took some pictures during our last Diwali celebration," Hritesh responded. He quickly scurried off, sifted through his desk drawers, and returned with a photograph. "Here you go," he said, placing the picture on the counter. Swati studied it, showed it to Nitya, and carefully slid it into her bag.

Nitya jumped when the large wall clock struck six. The library was about to close. She returned to the counter, where Bharat and Hritesh were shuffling back toward their desks.

"I am sorry, but we are closing. I think we have helped you as much as we could," Bharat said, to which Hritesh nodded.

Nitya offered them a smile. "Thank you, Bharat Ji, Hritesh Ji. What you have told us might help us find Dinesh Nath, and we will certainly keep you posted if we learn anything new. Meanwhile, if you think of anything else, please call us. Here are our names and contact numbers," Nitya said, scribbling the details on a piece of paper and handing it to Bharat.

He took it and then turned to the small crowd lined up at the counter, waiting to check out their books. Hritesh followed suit. As Nitya and Swati left the library, Nitya noticed that the old librarian kept sneaking glances at her and Swati.

They soon reached the street corner where Nitya's car was parked. She turned to her assistant, but Swati spoke first.

"Well, that's not at all what I was expecting. Dinesh Nath is missing, and it's even become a police matter. I am sure that if they'd found him, we would have known by now," Swati said.

Nitya nodded and added, "We could have gotten his family's address in Mussoorie. But I suspect the police are already looking into that."

Swati narrowed her eyes. "Do you think Bharat and Hritesh told us everything, ma'am?"

"I believe so," Nitya responded. "They don't have any reason to lie or mislead us."

"True." Swati drew a breath of cool winter air and straightened her shoulders. "So, where to next? We have this hotel address that the police are probably investigating. But we don't know where else he worked in Bombay."

"No, we don't. But..." Nitya locked eyes with Swati, a smile teasing her lips.

"But what, ma'am?"

"What do I keep telling our team? We have to keep digging. Journalism isn't always as glorious as it's made out to be. How many firms do you think there are in Andheri selling air coolers?" She raised an eyebrow.

"I have no idea," Swati responded, smiling. Swati must have guessed where this was leading.

"Well, let's find out. Start with the phone book. Remember, we are now part of *The Daily Citizen News*! We have a big office in Bombay, so let's contact them and have them do some legwork for us," Nitya suggested.

"Aren't you...?" Swati started.

"Yes, I am leaving for Bombay in two days to attend some leadership meetings. I'll do some digging myself if you can get me all the information before then. It will be a welcome change from all the politics and nonsense circling the Delhi office."

"Can I—" Swati blurted, but Nitya cut her off.

"I know what you are going to ask," she responded. "The answer is no. I need you here to follow up on this story and our leads in the narcotics case. I promise to keep you posted on what's going on in Bombay. You'll still be working with me on this," Nitya asserted. She could sense Swati's relief in hearing that.

"Thank you, ma'am. I will start compiling all the details right away," she gushed.

"No." Nitya's tone was final. "We have done enough for today. Leave it till tomorrow morning. Come, I will drop you off at home. I need to get back, too." She shook her head. "My sister must be fuming. I told her I'd be back by five to head out for dinner and a movie."

"It's fine. I can take the bus," Swati said.

"No way. I am still your boss, and this is just one of those orders you must obey," Nitya said, and they both laughed.

***

When Nitya finally entered her apartment, Kavita's voice rose from the living room. It sounded like she was on the phone with their parents. Nitya tiptoed into the kitchen without wanting to participate in the conversation. She overheard Kavita arguing with their mother. From Kavita's responses, it was obvious they were discussing the same old topic—their marital status.

Nitya sighed and quietly brewed herself some tea. A few minutes later, Kavita stormed into the kitchen, seething. Thankfully, her ire was directed toward their mother, not Nitya's tardiness.

"Mom's unbelievable," Kavita huffed, picking up her mug and sinking into the large sofa in the living room. That wasn't exactly news to Nitya. Still, she wanted to give her younger sister the chance to vent and let it all out.

"You know how she is," Nitya said, settling into the armchair beside the sofa and leaning back. "There's no point in arguing with her. Trust me, I know. As the eldest, I have already borne the brunt of her scoldings."

"Yeah, well, you did come up in our conversation," Kavita said.

Nitya raised an eyebrow. "Oh?"

"She told me not to end up like you. In your thirties, still single, working like crazy, going out with a much older professor, not wanting a family, et cetera, et cetera. You know the drill," Kavita replied, clutching her cup tighter.

"I'm well aware," sighed Nitya with a nod. "Well, she still has one daughter who is married and has kids. Her eldest and youngest may be single, but at least she has someone she can point to and be proud of."

"It's not just that," Kavita said. Nitya caught her sudden change in tone.

"What is it?" Nitya asked, angling herself to face Kavita.

"I think she's disappointed that my marriage didn't work out, and now that the divorce has finally come through, she views me as a failure," Kavita mumbled before falling silent.

Nitya got up and moved closer to sit beside Kavita, wrapping her arms around her. "I know it's been difficult, but it's not your fault. And you are *not* a failure. Just look at what you have accomplished since you came to Delhi. You've managed to finish a course, work in a reputed hotel as a manager, and are financially independent. That counts for a lot."

"Not in Mom's eyes. She'd be happier if I was still married, gave up my career to be a housewife, and had some kids," Kavita said, sniffling.

"I know." Nitya nodded. "But we can't change her opinion. The best you can do is to keep pursuing what makes you happy; with time, she will understand. Then again, maybe..."

"Maybe what?"

Nitya sighed. "Maybe it's time to tell her and Dad about Nalin," she said in a hushed tone. Nitya was the only one who knew about Nalin, a colleague at the hotel where Kavita worked. They had met a few months ago and instantly hit it off. Nitya had seen him a few times and thought him good-natured. What swayed her was that Kavita was happy with Nalin, who had been there for her when she needed a good friend. With Kavita's divorce finalised, they could now make plans for a future together. The budding relationship could also pacify their mother. But Kavita had held off discussing this with her parents.

"I know," Kavita said, resting her head on Nitya's shoulder. "I have been thinking about that. But there's something I haven't told you."

"What?" Nitya tried to sit up, but Kavita pressed her head into her shoulder more firmly to prevent her from doing so.

"Kavita, what is it? You are worrying me."

"It's just that ... Nalin hasn't told his parents everything about me," Kavita muttered.

"I don't understand. You have met his parents twice already, and I thought they knew their son was interested in you."

"They do. They don't know that I've been married before," Kavita blurted in a tumble of words before glancing away.

"What? Why not?"

"He doesn't know how they will take it. I know it's the '80s and all. And this is Delhi. But they come from a small town. You know very well that it's never easy for girls once they are divorced," Kavita added.

"I know all that, but I'm surprised and slightly disappointed in Nalin. He should have come clean with his parents concerning your past," Nitya said, leaning back on the sofa.

"To be fair, I haven't told our parents either," Kavita noted.

"True, but that's different. Your divorce hadn't come through yet. On top of that, Mom has been yearning for you to return to Bombay and give your marriage another shot. I think the time has come to tell them about Nalin, and you should insist that Nalin tell his parents everything about you. If you do choose to move forward, and if there are to be any hopes of a union, your relationship cannot be based on deception and half-truths," Nitya stated with authority, sitting upright and reaching for her cup on the coffee table.

"Oh, I don't know," sighed Kavita, plunging her head into Nitya's lap. "Why does this have to be so complicated? I didn't even want to talk about all this today. What took you so long? Now, it's too late for dinner and a movie."

"I know, sorry. It's just this weird story that fell into our lap. I'm not sure what it's all about," Nitya said, caressing Kavita's hair.

"Well, we can order in, and you can tell me all about it," Kavita said, sounding more upbeat.

"I'd rather not talk about work," Nitya mumbled. "But maybe there is something I can ask you since you spent some time in Bombay."

"What's that?"

"About Andheri and air coolers," Nitya said.

"Now you're talking nonsense," Kavita said with a smile. "Andheri is a neighbourhood in Bombay—a good one at that. It's a posh place, parts of it anyway. I don't know what it has to do with air coolers."

"Well, it seems one of our contacts worked for an air cooler company in Andheri," Nitya explained.

"Ah, so that's what you're getting at. I'm sure there can't be too many stores that sell air coolers there. I only know of one large showroom in Andheri, where we went looking for an air cooler when we first moved to Bombay. If you want, I can look up the address in the phone book," Kavita said, getting up.

"Not right now. Let's not talk about my work, your work, or Nalin," Nitya said with a yawn.

"Let me order some food, then." Kavita sprang to her feet and started shuffling through a mess of flyers on the kitchen table.

"Sure." Nitya nodded.

"Chinese?" Kavita asked, holding a flyer to Nitya, who was still lounging on the sofa.

"Sounds good."

Kavita picked up the phone and started rattling off a slew of dishes. Once she hung up, she returned to where Nitya was seated and planted herself in the armchair.

"How are things going with the professor?"

"Oh, I should have added that to the list of things I don't

want to discuss," Nitya groaned.

"What happened? Did you fight?" Kavita leaned forward with interest.

"No," sighed Nitya. "We don't talk much anymore, so I'm unsure exactly where we stand. He is busy, and so am I. It's difficult to find time for one another, and..."

"And what?" Kavita pressed.

"Well, sometimes I find reasons to stay busy at work, and I prioritise that over spending time with Jai," Nitya said, averting her gaze.

"That doesn't sound good. Are you sure there wasn't an argument or a fight?"

"No. It sounds silly, but I think we have gotten bored of each other. Even when we meet up, we hardly talk. I don't know. I can't put my finger on it. He is a good guy, and he doesn't pressure me into anything. But ..."

"Are you two still interested in one another? I mean, this is the first time you've told me this," Kavita said, scooting closer.

"I think so, but you see, he was away at some conference, and I can't say I missed him. Even after he came back, I didn't feel the urge to see him," Nitya remarked. "Isn't that strange? If I really liked him, I'd want us to be together more often, and I'd certainly find some time for him."

"True." Kavita twisted a loose tendril of hair thoughtfully. "Seems you need to have a heart-to-heart talk with him. Does he feel the same way?"

"I don't know. He calls me more often than I call him, and he's the one who usually plans our outings. Or, at least, he did. But I think he is making less effort, partly because I keep making excuses to turn him down," Nitya said.

"I don't know what to tell you," Kavita said abruptly.

"Well, all that to say, there's one thing I do agree with Mom on. Do not take relationship advice from me. Here I am in my thirties, still single, and I seem to run away from anyone who wants to get close to me," Nitya said with a smirk, which made Kavita laugh.

"You are right about Nalin, though. I need to tell our parents about him, and he needs to tell his parents about my past," Kavita said.

As Nitya nodded her agreement, there was a knock on the door. Kavita jumped to her feet, grabbed her purse from the side table, and opened the door to receive the takeout they had ordered. Within minutes, they were seated around the small dining table and spent the rest of the evening talking about relationships, politics, cricket, and Bollywood. Nitya couldn't have asked for a better night.

***

When Nitya arrived in Bombay, she was struck by how different the city was from Delhi. Buildings were clustered relatively close, but navigating the crowded streets and bumper-to-bumper traffic took an eternity. The throng of travellers at Bombay's Central Station was impressive and scary. Everyone seemed focused on where they were headed, and no one seemed to mind the occasional jostling as the sea of humanity streamed toward their destinations.

Outside the station, a colourful array of cars, vans, buses, scooters, and bicycles dominated every inch of the road. Compared to Delhi, the vehicles' honks blared louder, and the people were always in a hurry. The never-ending constellation of street vendors and eateries made Nitya wonder if Bombay locals ate out more than they did in Delhi. Once the yellow-and-black Ambassador arrived at the towering news building, Nitya paid her taxi fare and hustled to the top floor.

One thing this city had in common with Delhi was the vibe and uncertainty at *The Daily Citizen News*. Between her mandatory meetings, Nitya gleaned that folks here were also worried about their jobs and bosses. And no one seemed too thrilled with the merger of the two papers. She was relieved to leave the office in the afternoon, so she visited Andheri for a quick lunch before chasing down Dinesh Nath's employer. Sitting down at a café, she ordered a vada pao and masala tea. As she bit into the steaming potato dumpling wrapped in a soft bun, she read through the folder that Swati had prepared for her.

Swati had managed a fair bit of research. After calling multiple showrooms and repair shops that dealt with air coolers, she could trace the one that had employed Dinesh Nath. The attendant Swati had spoken to at Golden Cooling Solutions had no idea of Dinesh's whereabouts except that he had moved to Delhi. Swati had also included a profile of the business owner, Mr Arvind Kapoor. Arvind was a well-known fixture in Bombay. In addition to his appliances showroom, he owned a small hotel near Juhu Beach.

Nitya examined the copies of newspaper cuttings that were included. They featured articles about Arvind's business, with photos of him and his employees. Even after studying them carefully, Nitya couldn't spot Dinesh in the pictures.

Once she finished her meal, she decided to walk the rest of the way to the showroom. The stroll helped her clear her head, and she realised how much she'd missed this. Ever since taking up a management role, she rarely did much legwork, leaving most of it to her team of journalists.

As she turned onto the boulevard where the showroom was located, Nitya noticed the traffic jam that stretched the road length. She double-checked the address and asked a street vendor, who pointed her to a large building less than fifty meters away.

When she approached the building, she realised the traffic had reached a standstill. Nitya moved closer to get a better look. A few meters from the building, a police barricade prevented anyone from entering or leaving the premises. A crowd had gathered outside, and Nitya could make out a group of onlookers and reporters trying to get the attention of the police.

"What's going on here?" Nitya asked a well-dressed gentleman.

"Absolute nonsense, if you ask me," came the brusque response, which startled Nitya.

"I'm sorry," Nitya said, glancing at him.

"I live in this building, and they won't let me in. They claim they have to secure the crime scene. Wonder how they'll manage that with all those constables trampling around," the old man huffed before turning to her. "Are you one of those pesky reporters?"

"I was here to meet someone at the showroom," Nitya replied, turning away from him and straining her neck to get a better look.

"Well, that's always been the bane of this building. I had written to the owners, warning them not to rent it to that company. Although it's a residential building, I understand that the ground floor was meant for stores and shops. But why did they have to rent it out to Golden Cooling Solutions, a business owned by that uncouth fellow?" The old man hissed. "And now look what's happened."

"I am sorry, sir, but what exactly has happened?" Nitya tilted her head to lock eyes with the old man, who was now gazing straight at her.

"Why do you think the whole circus is here?" he grumbled, pointing to the police barricade. "It's that scoundrel, Arvind Kapoor. He was murdered. Or maybe it was a suicide, but I doubt it. His body was found hanging in the showroom this morning."

Kin

Shankar was eager to see his son. Vikram was growing up fast, and after some initial hurdles, he had finally settled into his new school in Dehradun. It didn't hurt that his mother, Rohini, was a teacher there. Shankar and Rohini had come to a mutual understanding about how often Vikram would go to Delhi. Although Rohini never mentioned a formal separation, Shankar knew it was on her mind.

The two days he spent with Vikram in the Himalayan foothills made him forget everything at work. But Rohini, for her part, seemed more distant than usual. Although they were always cordial, she avoided lengthy conversations with him this time, and she would often leave him and Vikram alone to spend time together. *Is she seeing someone?* Shankar wondered. She seemed happier than usual. Although that had initially bothered Shankar, he slowly came to accept that, eventually, it would happen once they moved apart.

After his brief stay in Dehradun, Shankar headed to Mussoorie to visit Dinesh Nath's parents. The winding road through the Himalayas, with snow-capped peaks looming in the distance, reminded him of his childhood and happier times with Rohini and Vikram. He often wondered whether things would have turned out differently had he not moved to Delhi.

Pushing the thoughts from his mind, he stopped briefly to have some tea and chat with the officers at the local station. Then, he climbed back into his Jeep and navigated to the address on the paper Ashok had given him.

Shankar parked outside the small bungalow, an overgrown garden peeking out from the narrow front yard. The home was perched near the top of a hill amid many such structures in the crowded neighbourhood. The narrow streets were steep and unpaved, but the surroundings stole his breath away, with groves of towering trees standing beneath the ever-present peaks of the majestic Himalayas. The bitter wind bit into his skin and stung his throat, and people in the street hurried to their destinations wrapped in heavy jackets, coats, or shawls. Before passing through the rickety metal gates, Shankar turned to survey the area. A few neighbours watched him with inquisitive eyes, which was to be expected. A policeman in uniform was not too common in this area. He smiled back and dipped his head to them to put them at ease. A few nodded back, and others turned their heads quickly and rushed back into their homes.

The bungalow's squeaky gate alerted the occupants, and soon, Shankar was met by an older gentleman who seemed to be having some trouble locating his glasses in the pocket of his coat. When he did, he stared at Shankar, blinking, and pointed to the front door. They went inside, and Shankar sat down on a chair in the small living room. Everything inside was dark and damp. After exchanging pleasantries, the old man sat across from Shankar and rubbed his hands to warm them.

"Tea, sir?"

"Oh, no. That's quite all right," Shankar said.

"I am having one anyway. Are you sure?" the man pressed.

Shankar smiled. "Well, in that case ..."

"Wonderful." The old man got up and scurried into the next room, giving Shankar time to look around. The sparsely furnished room desperately needed a coat of paint. The dining table and bookcases were coated in a fine layer of dust, and the only window in the room was firmly shut with the curtains drawn. Some photographs were hung on the wall, but when scanning them, he couldn't find any of Dinesh Nath. After a moment, the man re-entered and settled into his chair.

"Were you aware that I would be showing up?" Shankar asked, keeping his tone subdued and polite.

"Yes," the old man replied. "A constable from the local station came by to announce that someone from Delhi would be stopping here to gather more information about Dinesh. I am Dinesh's father, Nikhil."

"Nikhil Ji, I'll try not to take up much of your time. You see, Dinesh's colleagues at the library, where he works as a security guard, asked for my help when they hadn't heard from him for over a week. I was hoping you'd know where we might find him," Shankar said.

"That's strange," Nikhil mumbled, stroking his chin. "I never knew he worked at the library. He always told me he worked at a warehouse on the outskirts of Delhi. I'm afraid that's all I know."

"Perhaps the name of the warehouse?" Shankar prodded.

"Unfortunately, he never mentioned the name. All I know is that the place is used for storing and transporting appliances," Nikhil continued.

Before Shankar could ask his next question, an elderly woman came by with a tray of tea and biscuits. Shankar stood up to greet her with folded hands. She smiled and gestured for him to sit. After introducing herself as Dinesh's mother, she poured them some tea and left the room.

Shankar took a sip, and the piping hot tea brought a wave of welcome warmth. Although he was bundled up, the cool dampness in the room was cutting through to his bones. They both fell silent to enjoy the tea, and Shankar took the opportunity to consider the man before him. Nikhil had an easy disposition, but he was hard to read and wasn't offering much by way of details. What unsettled Shankar most was that Nikhil kept bouncing his knees, only occasionally making eye contact when he spoke. Shankar decided to press the issue another way.

"Though we can't be sure, Nikhil Ji, we suspect Dinesh may be in danger. The fact that no one knows his whereabouts doesn't usually bode well for anyone. Can you give us anything that might point us in the right direction?" Shankar asked, choosing his words carefully.

The old man's eyes widened, his jaw trembling slightly. He darted his gaze toward the other room before getting up and leaving. Shankar could hear bits and pieces of an animated conversation between Nikhil and his wife. Then, after a few minutes, he emerged, clutching a sheet of paper.

"I am not sure if this helps," Nikhil started, handing the sheet to Shankar. "It's the address of his wife's family in Delhi."

"Oh, that will certainly help," Shankar said. He glanced at the paper and tucked it between the pages of the large notebook he always carried.

"You see, we never kept in touch with him after he married that woman," scoffed Nikhil. The abrupt transformation in his demeanour and tone caught Shankar off guard. "She destroyed him."

"How so?" Shankar asked before hastily adding, "If you don't mind my asking."

"As soon as he got involved with her, Dinesh became distant, aloof. I think she never wanted him to have a good relationship with us. Things only went downhill from there."

"'Her,' as in ..."

"Sanaya," huffed Nikhil. "That's her name."

"Where did they meet?" Shankar went on.

"In Bombay. Dinesh worked at a hotel and then a showroom for a couple of years. That's where they met," Nikhil said, his tone still tinged with bitterness.

"Has she contacted you?"

"Of course not! Why should she? We don't want anything to do with her," Nikhil snapped, shaking his head.

"Why?"

"What do you mean?" the old man demanded, glowering.

"I mean, what is it about her that convinced you not to get to know her?" Shankar asked, his tone still soft.

"That's enough!" Nikhil huffed. An uncomfortable silence stretched between them. A noise in the adjoining room broke it. As Nikhil shifted his gaze toward the sound, Shankar studied him.

"Have you met her?" he pressed, not wanting to switch topics.

"Only once, when Dinesh brought her home to introduce her," Nikhil responded hurriedly.

"I don't understand." Shankar took another sip and gently placed the cup back on the table. "Didn't you see her at the wedding?"

"No!" Nikhil snapped, once again visibly fuming at the suggestion. "They had a court marriage, and that was that."

"Where did they register their marriage?"

"In Delhi," sneered Nikhil. "I am sure when you meet her parents, *they* can give you more details."

"Certainly, Nikhil Ji. We will get in touch with them," Shankar said. "Can I ask you for another favour?"

He sat back, reining in his outburst. "Of course, sir."

"Could you give me the addresses of the hotel and the company that Dinesh worked for in Bombay?" Shankar asked.

"Really?" Nikhil blinked back, his eyes wide. "I am surprised you don't know that already. Dinesh told me he was required to share all his details with you."

Shankar scrutinised the old man through narrowed eyes. "I am sorry, I don't understand. You're saying we should have all his details?"

His question was met with complete silence. Nikhil got up slowly, hobbled toward the window, and turned around to face Shankar. "When you first arrived, I thought you were coming to share his whereabouts. You'd tell us not to worry and that he is off on one of his many trips, like in the past."

"I am at a loss, Nikhil Ji. What makes you believe that we would know his travel plans?" Shankar demanded.

Nikhil's brow wrinkled. "Because he's employed by you. He is a police informer. Didn't you know that?"

***

The moment Shankar returned to Delhi, he immediately sent for Ashok. His trusted assistant arrived, and Shankar asked him to sit across his table. He then rattled off everything he had learned in Mussoorie. When he finished, Ashok intertwined his fingers before his mouth as if trying to make sense of the missing pieces. After a long minute, his questions tumbled out.

"Wow! If he is a police informer, shouldn't we have known about it?"

"That depends. If it were a cross-border narcotics case, we would have known. If it were something else, then no, not necessarily," contended Shankar.

"Was the local station in Mussoorie aware?"

"No," Shankar affirmed.

Ashok nodded slowly, looking thoughtful. "What about this little girl? Does he have a daughter, as we suspected?"

"Not that Dinesh's father knew of. I mean ... why would he hide such a thing?" Shankar wondered aloud.

"True, sir." Ashok studied his notepad, having taken a number of rushed notes during Shankar's monologue. He turned the page and stared at his scrawl. "This is an intriguing case. But what are we investigating, exactly? A missing person? No one seems to care that he has vanished."

"You have a point. But something's not right here, and I can't put my finger on it. For the sake of argument, let's say that Dinesh truly is a police informer and has gone missing. Then, someone in the station must know," Shankar suggested.

"There's still the possibility that he's on some sort of trip," Ashok uttered hesitantly.

"If that were the case, why not tell someone? You'd think that, at the very least, he'd let his family and employer at the library know to avoid arousing any suspicion, especially if he is working with the authorities. This is a basic protocol that every informant is drilled with," Shankar said, folding his hands over the desk.

Ashok nodded. "Anything else that strikes you as odd?"

"Yes," Shankar muttered.

"What, sir?"

"Two things. There were no pictures of Dinesh on the walls of his parents' home—the house where he grew up. I spotted photos of his parents and siblings, but none with him," Shankar stated.

"Maybe that's because they were upset with him for marrying this ..." Ashok shuffled his notepad and glanced at it. "Sanaya."

"That is a possible explanation, but it's a stretch if you ask me. You may not get along with your kids, but you would still have their photos displayed," Shankar said, looking past Ashok to the far end of the room.

"And the second thing that struck you, sir?"

"They were not very forthcoming when it came to Dinesh. Initially, I thought they didn't know. But now, I am convinced that it's something else." Shankar sat back, puzzling over the whole encounter.

"Why would that be? If he is missing, wouldn't they want to give you as much information as possible to help you track him down?" Ashok remarked.

"See, that's the thing. I didn't get the impression that they truly believe he is missing. In the past, he has gone off the radar for days without letting them know. It could well be that this is one of those instances. Nevertheless ..."

"Sir?" Ashok pressed, his brow furrowed. "What makes you think otherwise?"

"I believe they were scared of something." Shankar locked eyes with his constable.

"Scared of what?"

"I am not sure. I tried to ask Dinesh's father whether they had been threatened, but I didn't get a straight answer. Then, he suddenly fell quiet," Shankar noted.

"Who might have threatened them? The gang Dinesh runs with? Or maybe the ones his handler is investigating. Could they have found out he was an insider?"

"I am not sure. If that were the case, he would have tried to say something, but then ..." Shankar trailed off.

"If not the gang, then who else could it have been?" Ashok continued.

Shankar fixed his eyes on Ashok. "Nikhil didn't want to tell a *policeman*. That could well be because he doesn't trust us, or ..."

"Or it was the police who threatened him?" Ashok thundered.

Shankar shrugged. "Maybe I am reading too much into this.

I don't know." He drew a heavy sigh.

"Where do we go from here, sir?" Ashok glanced at his notebook and then at Shankar.

"Right. So, I'd like to talk to Sanaya and her parents. But they live in Old Delhi. With everything that's going on with the narcotics case and its aftermath, there is no way I can find time today. I want you to meet with them and see if you can get more info from Dinesh's wife," Shankar said, then paused.

"Understood, sir," Ashok said with a dip of his chin.

"And before you go, I want you to do a couple of things. First, find out whether Dinesh Nath has a record—anything at all: petty theft, burglary, et cetera. Then, do the same for Sanaya. I doubt you'll find much, but it's worth checking."

"Will do, sir."

"Next, pass by the registrar's office and check whether Dinesh and Sanaya are married. With every turn, this case seems to spring new surprises and more questions than answers. I want to ensure we don't take anything for granted," Shankar added.

"Makes sense, sir," Ashok said.

"And one last thing." Shankar glanced at the door, checking that it was firmly shut.

"Sir?"

"Let's keep this between us. I don't want anyone in the station to catch wind of what we're doing."

"Agreed, sir," Ashok mumbled, his eyes flitting to the door.

"All right, off you go. We will meet at the club in the evening, and you can tell me all about it," Shankar said with a smile.

Ashok stood up, nodded, and marched out of the room. Shankar got up from his chair and shuffled over to the window, opening it wide to let the sunlight stream in. He watched as officers and constables went about their business on the outer grounds.

Looking more closely, he noticed a smaller convoy of vans, Jeeps, and trucks than usual. Yet, there were no raids planned. He kept his eyes on the grounds, and after a minute or so, he saw Ashok getting into his Jeep and instructing his driver on where to go.

The phone rang at Shankar's desk, drawing him away. He quickly picked it up, only to learn he was late for a meeting. He gathered the files on his desk and strode to the end of the corridor to meet with his peers and their boss, Gagan Singh.

When he entered the meeting room, Shankar realised he was the last to arrive. He nodded to the rest of the officers and apologised quietly. No one seemed too bothered, returning to the usual small talk that preceded such meetings. Shankar decided to keep quiet, sitting back and observing all the officers. After a moment, his eyes fell on Gagan, the highest-ranking officer at the station for nearly six years. He seemed in good spirits.

Soon, the meeting was underway, opening with lengthy discussions on how the raids could have been carried out more effectively. Raids constantly strained resources, and the Home Ministry was always wary of approving and disbursing funds unless there was something concrete to warrant them. That put considerable pressure on Shankar and his colleagues, who were forced to justify the raids. If they didn't yield the desired results, subsequent requests were scrutinised.

Thankfully, Shankar hadn't been the one to order the raids, and he was still in Gagan's and his superiors' good graces. But after the issues he'd caused with his bosses in the past, he was wary of involving them unless he had to.

The meeting lasted nearly three hours, with a few breaks in between. The team eventually concluded that the operation on the outskirts of Delhi had been partially successful. No one mentioned that someone inside the police station might have been a mole. Shankar was convinced that his fellow officers would save that conversation for when they spoke one-on-one with Gagan.

When the meeting concluded, Gagan requested that Shankar stay back. After everyone filed out, he asked Shankar to join him on the sofa in the corner of the spacious meeting room.

"Oh, these are so much more comfortable," Gagan said, sinking into the sofa as he sighed.

"Yes, sir," Shankar replied with a smile.

"Nasty business, these raids. I have already received calls from the Home Secretary on how much we've spent and whether they were justified," Gagan continued.

"They were, sir." Shankar sat up straighter. "Any drugs and dealers we take off the streets is a win. Don't you think?"

"Oh, yes. Trust me, I am with you on this. But what bothers me is the question we were discussing earlier today. Why didn't our raids yield a bigger haul? All of us went round and round without actually providing any answers. Don't you agree?" Gagan leaned forward slightly, his eyes sharp.

"I think the answer lies in what was not discussed in today's meeting," Shankar responded, knowing full well what Gagan was alluding to.

"That someone in the department may be on the payroll of the drug-smuggling masterminds," stated Gagan in a solemn tone.

"Either that or we were incredibly unlucky. And I don't think that's the case," Shankar remarked.

Gagan hummed thoughtfully. "Tell me, why haven't you come to me with this hunch?" he asked, rubbing his chin. "Some of your fellow officers have already confided their suspicions to me privately."

"Because there was nothing to show for it, sir. Hurling accusations within the department is a tricky business. I'd rather not discuss this until I know whether there is a mole and who is involved," Shankar declared.

"Understood, Shankar," Gagan said. Neither man spoke for a while, but Shankar noticed Gagan watching him. When their eyes met, he smiled and looked away.

"Is this something you want me to look into, sir?"

"Hmm," Gagan murmured, staring at the files on his desk. "What's that?"

"The theory about a mole in this station," Shankar said. His boss kept his gaze on his desk and slowly turned to him.

"Not at the moment. Perhaps you can make discreet inquiries if you know what I mean. But do keep me apprised of any new developments, as you always do," Gagan said, sitting upright.

"Developments on what, sir?"

"On this and anything else you might be working on," Gagan continued.

Shankar nodded slowly, somewhat surprised by the odd request. "Certainly, sir."

"You know, it was strange. During the meeting, I noticed everyone's constables stopped by to inform them about their calls and schedules. But I didn't see Ashok. Where is he?"

Once again, the comment caught Shankar off guard. This wasn't something a person in Gagan's rank usually noticed, much less brought up. Shankar hesitated before responding.

"I sent him on an errand, sir. Nothing too important. I knew I'd be busy in these meetings all day, so I figured that'd give him time to finish some pending work," Shankar replied, choosing each word carefully. Gagan's expression softened, and he smiled.

"Of course. We are all busy, and we'll need to be on our toes with everything going on. At least for the foreseeable future," Gagan said, slowly getting up. That was the cue for Shankar to take his leave. Standing from the sofa, he headed for the door and hesitated, turning back to Gagan. But before Shankar could say anything,

Gagan's phone started ringing. His boss then launched into a conversation with the minister at the other end of the line. After exchanging a wave and a nod with his preoccupied boss, Shankar dragged his feet back to his office, his mind brewing with questions.

***

When Shankar arrived at the Officer's Club, the venue was tranquil. Winter evenings usually meant a steady flow of officers and their wives enjoying drinks and food at the indoor lounge or the restaurant. Shankar usually parked himself at the bar next to the library. He liked to unwind by paging through magazines in the reading room and having a drink before heading home. Tonight, he saw all the usual faces at the bar. A few patrons were lined up near the kebab station at the far end, eager for some fresh mutton and chicken tikkas. It wasn't long before Ashok strode into the club, receiving glares from some officers.

Usually, head constables didn't enter the club unless they were invited. When the officers noticed Ashok shuffling toward Shankar, they looked away. Shankar waved Ashok over, staring down some of his colleagues who were tossing snide remarks at Ashok as he passed. Shankar motioned to a set of upholstered seats in a corner with a round table between them, and they settled in. Ashok was still casting glances at the other patrons in the bar. But Shankar didn't care. He knew that the club was now open to all, although only his colleagues in the officer cadre showed up in practice.

"Never mind them," Shankar said. "The ones who were staring have been here for a while and have had too much to drink."

"Right, sir," Ashok mumbled, glimpsing the intoxicated man struggling to sit upright at the other end of the bar.

"You have been here before, haven't you?"

"Yes, sir. Usually, it's a bit more crowded, and there are more families," Ashok replied.

Shankar nodded. "Well, Delhi winters. What else can I say?"

"But sir ..."

"You are not in uniform or on duty, so go ahead. I don't mind," Shankar cut in, hailing a passing waiter. Once Ashok ordered a whiskey and some kebabs, Shankar tried to put him at ease, asking about things unrelated to work. After a few minutes, Ashok leaned back in his chair, looking more relaxed.

The drinks arrived, and they enjoyed a few sips before Ashok placed a file and notepad on the table. He sifted through the pages until he arrived at one with markings scribbled on it.

"Let's start with the simpler question, sir."

"Whether Dinesh Nath is married?" Shankar confirmed.

Ashok nodded. "At the registrar's office, I did verify that Dinesh Nath and Sanaya Joshi were indeed married five years ago."

"All right, so they may have a child whose abacus we found at Dinesh's apartment."

"Well, that's where things get interesting. Before I come to that, I wanted to tell you what happened at the Joshi residence while I was looking for Sanaya," Ashok said, taking a big gulp from his glass.

"Please, go ahead." Shankar angled his body toward Ashok, giving his assistant his undivided attention.

"Sanaya's parents are retired government employees. They used to work in the Delhi Municipal Corporation and own a small apartment in Old Delhi, where Dinesh and his family live. The house is nothing spectacular, and they seemed surprised that I showed up at their doorstep looking for their son-in-law." Ashok paused, his lips tightening into a thin line.

"What do you mean?" Shankar pressed, leaning forward.

"From their perspective, Sanaya and Dinesh took off on a trip to Rajasthan a few days ago," Ashok continued.

"What, why? And what about this girl?" demanded Shankar.

"The girl, Aria, is indeed their daughter, but she is adopted."

"Adopted?" Shankar wrinkled his brow.

"Yes, sir."

"Why did they leave for Rajasthan?"

"One day, Sanaya told them that Aria's birth parents wanted to meet her, and Dinesh and Sanaya left in a hurry, taking her to meet them," Ashok said.

"Why the urgency, and why now? Isn't that a bit strange?" Shankar asked, folding his arms.

"That's not all," Ashok continued, but Shankar lifted a palm to stop him.

"Before you go on, did anyone see them travelling together? Did these folks witness Aria, Sanaya, and Dinesh heading to Rajasthan?"

"Not quite, sir. You see, Sanaya's parents have an ancestral home in Jaisalmer. According to her parents, Sanaya called in a hurry and mentioned she was taking Aria and Dinesh to a village near Jaisalmer. And you are right, sir; it was all very sudden. The keys had been left with a neighbour when Sanaya's parents arrived to take care of their apartment," Ashok said before reaching for his glass to finish his drink.

"Did Sanaya tell them how long they would be away?"

Ashok shook his head.

"Something's not adding up," Shankar muttered. "Do Dinesh's in-laws know where they are going in Rajasthan, the address of Aria's birth parents?"

"No, sir. They could only tell me that Sanaya's family was headed to Jaisalmer. I also asked them about the adoption certificate. Although they searched for it around the house while I was there, they couldn't locate it. They promised to contact me if they found the papers or heard back from Sanaya or Dinesh," Ashok said with a firm nod.

"Do you believe them?"

"Yes, sir. I believe they are clueless as to Sanaya's whereabouts. They were surprised at her sudden departure and are now in the dark."

"But you did get the address of Sanaya's ancestral home in Jaisalmer," Shankar confirmed.

"Yes, sir." Ashok locked eyes with him. "And before you ask, I called the Jaisalmer police station to send a constable there and let me know if the house is occupied. They will get back to me tomorrow."

"Hmm." Shankar leaned back, closing his eyes. The image of the storekeeper from his dream flashed before him, making his scalp prickle. His eyes shot open to see Ashok tilting back his newly refilled glass and gulping down his whiskey. "What about the other thing?"

"What's that, sir?" Ashok reached for a napkin and wiped his mouth.

"The police record?"

"Ah. I was getting to that. But no—nothing on either Dinesh or Sanaya. At least, not yet. But I will keep looking," Ashok affirmed.

"Good work, Ashok," Shankar said. "What about Dinesh? What do his in-laws know about him?"

Ashok's eyes gleamed. "That's the interesting part." Before he could continue, a plateful of kebabs arrived. They paused their conversation and helped themselves to the sizzling meat. After a few bites, Shankar pressed Ashok again.

"Let's start with Dinesh. What did the Joshis tell you about him?"

"Sanaya met Dinesh in Bombay, where he worked in a hotel and then at a showroom. Sanaya was living with her brother's family as she pursued higher studies. They decided to marry and move back to Delhi—not because of Dinesh, but because of Sanaya's job," Ashok said. He opened his mouth to continue, but Shankar cut him off.

"Let's stay focused on Dinesh, shall we? Did they know about this warehouse or the library?"

"They confirmed that he works as a security guard in a warehouse in Gurgaon. But they don't know which one. Only that it stores appliances."

"What about his weekend work as a night guard?" Shankar continued.

"That was news to them. They also didn't know that Dinesh had a separate apartment near the library. They seemed shocked about that."

"So, as far as they knew, Dinesh lives with Sanaya and Aria in the apartment in Old Delhi," Shankar said before taking another sip.

"Yes," Ashok confirmed.

"Well, we could visit a few warehouses in Gurgaon with Dinesh's photograph. It may take some time, but we should be able to locate his workplace," Shankar mused aloud. "As for Aria's birth parents, we could contact the adoption agencies. Maybe they can shed light on their identities, although that may require a court order."

"Right, sir."

"All right. Now, let's move on to Sanaya. What's so interesting about her?"

"After she graduated, she lived in Bombay for a while, working in different places." Ashok opened another file and pulled out a photograph of Sanaya, Dinesh, and Aria. He handed it to Shankar.

After examining it carefully, he gave it back to Ashok. "That's a nice picture. One happy family, I'd say. And it was taken in Bombay. You can see the Gateway of India in the back."

"Right, sir. Sanaya's parents told me that they were indeed a happy family. Then, something changed six months ago," Ashok murmured as he reread his notes.

"Around the time Dinesh started working in the library and rented out an apartment in Bharat's building," Shankar remarked.

"That's right, sir."

"What else?"

"As I said, they moved back to Delhi because of Sanaya's job. You see, she is one of us," Ashok declared. Before he could explain, Shankar froze.

"What do you mean, one of us?"

"She is a policewoman. Not from the officer cadre, but a havildar in the Rajasthan Police," Ashok said with practised calm.

"What!"

"That's not all, sir. I got the details of her station in Bhiwadi, Rajasthan, near here, and what she is currently working on." Ashok showed Shankar the notes he had jotted down during his visit to Sanaya's residence. He paused while Shankar scanned the notes, reading and rereading them. Then, Ashok slid a photo across the table. It was Sanaya, in uniform, in front of the Bhiwadi Police Station.

"Wow! This is certainly unexpected," Shankar said, handing the photograph back to Ashok. He shifted forward, placing his hands on the table. "So, Dinesh is an informer—or at least, that's what his father told us—and Sanaya is a member of the Rajasthan

Police. And they have an adopted daughter, Aria."

"That's correct, sir. When I called her station in Bhiwadi, I couldn't speak to her boss, but one of her colleagues said she was on leave due to a family emergency. Sanaya told her colleagues she would return in a couple of weeks. She didn't inform them where she was going, but they assumed it concerned her parents. But her mother and father seemed in perfect health this morning. The Joshis did tell me that it was highly uncharacteristic for either Sanaya or Dinesh to leave like this. They are worried about their daughter and her family," Ashok continued.

"Right," Shankar murmured. He slowly picked up the glass and took a sip, breathing a long sigh. "What is she working on? As a havildar, I am guessing it's the day-to-day issues that come to any police station," Shankar said. As the words left his mouth, Ashok's demeanour changed. The constable tapped his feet, fidgeting with his pen. Shankar gave him a pointed look. "Ashok, what is it?"

"I'll know more when I speak to her boss tomorrow, but I think it would be best if we paid a visit to Bhiwadi and met him in person," Ashok said, turning a page in his notebook.

"Yes, maybe after we check out the warehouses and adoption agencies. But please, go on. Tell me what you learned."

A moment passed before he spoke. "Sir, her parents revealed that she had taken on a new assignment that required her to travel across Rajasthan. They didn't have all the details, but from what they divulged, she seems part of a task force looking into gang activity."

Shankar's blood ran cold. "What sort of gang?"

"Smuggling, or at least, that's what they concluded from the little Sanaya had shared with them."

"All right. What about her colleague at the Bhiwadi Police Station?" Shankar asked.

"That's why I think we need to visit Bhiwadi. The colleague was rather coy and didn't give me much over the phone. I got the feeling that he knew, but he was wary of sharing the details," Ashok continued.

"So, nothing much to discuss on that front," Shankar said, rubbing his chin.

"Not quite, sir," Ashok mumbled. When Shankar looked up, he noticed Ashok darting glances around the room.

"Something's bothering you," Shankar said, leaning forward.

"No, sir. Uh—I mean—yes, sir. It's just what I uncovered about what she is working on, or rather, who she is working with," Ashok muttered before falling silent.

"What is it? Just tell me," Shankar demanded, leaving no room for argument.

"Sanaya's colleague told me that her task force is being led by the Delhi Police, and it involves multiple state and central agencies."

Shankar blinked back, puzzled. "But then, we would have known about it," he asserted. "Is she working undercover or something?"

"Her colleague didn't say so in as many words, but that's what I could deduce. We can confirm that easily if we speak to him in person."

Shankar nodded. "And we can learn the name of her handler. Maybe they can help us locate Sanaya," Shankar said, then paused, noticing that Ashok had gone quiet. "But that's not what's bothering you, is it?"

"No, sir." Ashok cleared his throat. "When we started talking, I told him my name, where I work, and other details—the proper thing to do. He told me that Sanaya's handler, or rather, the person she interacts with for this task force, is someone in our station. He didn't know the officer's name because Sanaya never mentioned it. But he is certain that it is one of your colleagues."

Shroud

Calling her office in Delhi, Nitya announced that she would spend the rest of the week in Bombay. Next, she rang Swati, recounting everything she'd learned before asking her to dig up more details on the late Arvind Kapoor's family and businesses.

When she asked Swati to join her in Bombay, she could hear the excitement in her assistant's voice. Upon her arrival, she was to meet Nitya at the guesthouse where she was staying. In the meantime, Nitya decided to swing by the deceased businessman's hotel to see what she could learn.

Arvind Kapoor's hotel on Juhu Beach wasn't the most lavish establishment in the area. But the area itself was among the city's most expensive and sought-after, attracting Bombay's rich and famous. Walking down Marine Drive along the Arabian Sea, Nitya took a deep breath of salty air. This restless metropolis was bursting at its seams, so different from her sleepy hometown of Callipur. She marvelled at the many languages that struck her ears as she meandered toward the crossing where the hotel was located. The streets and sidewalks were busy, but there was a reassuring flow to the movement. The warm air caressed her skin, a welcome change from the cold in Delhi.

The Grand Juhu Lodge located a block from the sea, was neither grand nor a lodge. The three-story structure looked more like a hostel built for students, backpackers, and budget-minded travellers. The ground floor housed two large restaurants with diners, a sprawling reception, and a lobby. Through the tall glass windows, Nitya spotted several travellers lounging on the colourful sofas, poring over open maps. The two upper floors reminded her of an apartment building, freshly painted in white. Some windows were open, with guests peering out to soak in the sun and marvel at the majestic avenue that showcased the coastline and the Arabian Sea beyond.

Nitya walked up to the young woman operating the reception desk. The woman looked up, smiled, and spoke before Nitya could say anything.

"Good afternoon, ma'am. Do you have a reservation at the lodge?"

"No. I was hoping to get something to eat at one of the restaurants. I also wanted to find out about someone who used to work here," Nitya responded.

"I'm not sure I can help. I haven't been here long, but perhaps our manager can answer your inquiries," the young woman said before adding, "You will find two restaurants here." She pointed to the two large doors on either side of the reception area. "One is a South Indian restaurant, and the other prepares mostly snacks and sandwiches."

"Which one's better?" Nitya asked with a smile.

The woman leaned closer. "The South Indian one. Their dosas are the best," came the hushed reply.

"All right. I will take your word for it," Nitya said. "Now, to the issue of my friend."

"Ah, yes. What's his name again?"

"Dinesh Nath," Nitya responded.

Nitya didn't miss the sudden change in the woman's demeanour as her face tightened. Before Nitya could continue, she stammered, "I think ... I-I don't know ..."

"Is everything all right?"

"Yes," the woman replied, quickly regaining her composure. "But I'm not sure if I can tell you more. I don't know much about this person you're referring to." Her tone was low and guarded.

"Then perhaps you can tell me whether Mr Chirag Seth works here. I believe he is the manager."

"Oh, yes," the woman replied, sounding relieved. "I'll go get him." With that, she disappeared into a room behind the reception. Nitya took the time to inspect the large lobby.

Photos of various landmarks around the city were displayed on the walls, and the establishment itself was clean and well-maintained. Before she could scrutinise it further, the young woman emerged from behind the door, followed by a short man with a bewildered expression. Running a hand over his bald head, he looked across the counter and locked eyes with Nitya.

"Good morning, ma'am. My name is Chirag Seth. How can I help you?"

Nitya offered a polite smile. "Namaste, Chirag Ji. My name is Nitya. I am here on a trip from Delhi. As I told your colleague, I wonder if you can help me locate Dinesh Nath."

"I am sorry, but who are you? I'm afraid we can't share that information," Chirag replied curtly.

"I know, but I haven't been in touch with him for a while. I was hoping you could assist me—"

"I am not in touch with him, nor has he contacted us," Chirag blurted, cutting her off. He bit his tongue and looked away before returning to Nitya. "Who are you? A friend?"

"More like a family acquaintance," Nitya said. She sensed that Chirag would bottle up immediately if he knew she was a reporter. "I spend a lot of time at the library where he works. I think you met him there a few months ago. Bharat Ji, the head librarian, told me that he hasn't heard from Dinesh and is concerned."

"Dinesh never mentioned you," Chirag continued, his eyes narrowing.

"I understand," Nitya said, not letting his wary undertone rattle her. "I don't want to get you in trouble. I am just trying to find him. It could be that he's just travelling and will be back soon. The thing is, Dinesh's family hasn't heard from him either. It's been more than a week, and they're worried. They knew I was coming to Bombay, so they asked me if I could contact his previous employers to inquire whether he has been in touch."

"I'm not sure how much more I can help," Chirag said, his voice softening. Then, he gestured to a line of guests behind Nitya waiting to check-in. "I am sorry, but as you can imagine, it's a busy time. We have to cater to our guests."

"Oh, that's all right. I appreciate your help. I'll enjoy some dosas in your restaurant and head to the police station. He is missing, after all, and they should be doing all this, in any case." She smiled at him, immediately witnessing Chirag's expression shift as she spun on her heel toward the restaurant.

She found a corner table facing Marine Drive, where she ordered a masala dosa and some tea. Sitting back, she waited, wondering what would happen first. Would the dosa arrive? Or would Chirag Seth show up before her *meal?* She turned her gaze toward the sea, and after a few minutes, Chirag eased himself into the chair across her table.

He looked around and nodded at a waiter, who scurried toward them. When the waiter stood at the ready, Chirag glanced at Nitya. "Have you ordered already, ma'am?"

"I have, Chirag Ji. If you want something, please go ahead," Nitya cooed. She studied Chirag's solemn expression as he hastily ordered some tea. Once the waiter left, he looked around to ensure they were out of earshot of the other patrons. He spoke in a hushed tone, his voice masked by the din of the bustling restaurant.

"Ma'am, it's not that I don't want to help, but there isn't much I can offer beyond what I've just told you. I knew Dinesh when he worked here, but he didn't keep in touch after he left."

"I understand. When he worked here, did he have any other friends or someone I could talk to who might know more?" Nitya reached into her bag to grab a notebook but decided against it.

"Well, he was friendly with all the staff. I don't recall anyone knowing him more than the others. He was happy working here, and then one day, he just left," Chirag said with a puzzled look.

"Why did he leave?"

"I'm not sure. He remained in Bombay but began working at an appliance store in Andheri. Mr Kapoor owns both this hotel and that store. We thought he may have asked Dinesh to transfer there, but ..."

"But what?" pressed Nitya

"I saw Dinesh a few months after he left the hotel, and that was the last time I saw him in Bombay. He seemed distant, unhappy. Sometime later, I heard he had moved to Delhi with his wife and daughter." Chirag stared out the window as he spoke, his brow furrowed.

"His wife and daughter?" Nitya said, resting her elbows on the table. Before Chirag could reply, their order arrived. Nitya tapped her fingers on the table as the waiter carefully laid out the dosa and tea. After he left, she continued, "Can you tell me more about them?"

"I figured you already knew? You said you were a family friend," Chirag started.

"Only through Bharat Ji, at the library where he works," Nitya said gingerly. "I don't know him personally. It is actually because of Bharat Ji that I am here. Dinesh never shared too many details with him," she quickly added.

"Yes, he was always that way, secretive, coy. I'm not sure why." Chirag nodded slowly, and Nitya took a deep breath, proceeding carefully.

"Anyway, can you tell me more about his wife and daughter?"

"Only that Sanaya, his wife, is from Delhi. She also used to work here in Bombay, and they have one daughter. She is adopted. I don't know much about either of them," Chirag said, reaching for his teacup and taking a sip.

"How did you contact him in Delhi? You saw him a few weeks ago. Did you know he worked at the library?"

Chirag's neck muscles tightened, his eyebrow twitching as he glanced away. A silence hung over them. Finally, he turned to Nitya. "No, I didn't know he worked at the library. When he moved, he only gave me his in-laws' address. That's where I wrote to him to say I would be in Delhi for a few days. He wrote back suggesting we meet in the evening at the library. I only discovered he worked there once I saw him in his uniform. He introduced me to the old librarian, and I could see that Bharat was fond of Dinesh. That's the only reason I am talking to you right now," Chirag said, then stopped.

"I understand, but—"

"That's it, Nitya ji. That's all I know, and that's all I can share," he snapped, cutting her off. "I've probably told you more than I should have." By his sharp tone, she could sense that he was angry. She wondered whether she should ask for the address of Dinesh's in-laws, but she decided against it. Chirag was already avoiding eye contact and sucking in short breaths. After another long pause, Nitya changed the subject.

"Are you sure you don't want to eat anything?" she asked, reaching for her dosa.

"I am fine, ma'am. Please, go ahead." Chirag folded his palms around his cup, regaining his composure.

After a couple of bites, Nitya realised how hungry she was. The masala dosa, a thin pancake filled with savoury potatoes and a generous portion of sambar, tickled her taste buds. As she chewed, she took the time to collect her thoughts. Halfway into her dosa, she paused and glanced at Chirag. He wore a pensive expression. "Chirag Ji, I want to thank you for your help. I'll try my best to locate Dinesh and let him know that you helped me find him."

"You can try the showroom in Andheri where he worked. I can give you the address," Chirag responded, easing himself out of his chair.

"I already have the address and will be going there as well," Nitya said.

"Well, visiting the showroom in person may be difficult. You see, Mr Kapoor passed away earlier this morning." Chirag's voice was solemn.

"Yes, I know. He was murdered, or so I heard." Nitya studied Chirag, but his expression didn't change.

"Well, I have heard it could be either." he turned his gaze to the large windows.

"Either?"

"Murder or suicide," Chirag uttered, facing Nitya again.

"Well, I suppose that's for the police to investigate," Nitya said before polishing off the rest of her dosa. Meanwhile, Chirag worked away at his tea, his eyes darting.

"I don't mean to sound evasive, but I've told you everything I know. If you go to the police, please try to keep our establishment out of it?" Chirag pleaded, tapping his fingertips on the edge of the table.

"I am not sure that will be possible. What I mean is, they will be coming here and questioning all of you anyway, in light of what happened to Mr Kapoor," Nitya said hurriedly.

Chirag nodded. "We are expecting that, but not in regards to Dinesh. It wouldn't bode well for the hotel's reputation if the police started investigating an ex-employee who had suddenly gone missing. And then ..."

Nitya fixed her eyes on him. "Then, what?"

"Then, there are those annoying press wallahs. A damn nuisance, I tell you. Irritating as hell," Chirag blurted, his lips curled in disgust.

"Ah, yes, those pesky reporters," Nitya said with a smile before drawing a sigh. "You need to watch out for them." Tilting back the last tea, she asked the waiter for the bill. Despite Chirag's insistence, she paid for both of them and then picked up her bag. Just before leaving, she turned to Chirag, who was slowly getting up.

"The last time you saw Dinesh in Bombay, when he was working at the store in Andheri, you mentioned that he didn't seem happy. I am guessing he never told you why?"

"No, ma'am. He only told me that he had befriended a guy, and it was the worst thing he'd ever done. This fellow had caused all sorts of trouble for him. Perhaps that was one of the reasons they decided to move to Delhi."

"He didn't give you a name?"

"No, only that he was a cunning fellow, and he regretted ever meeting him," Chirag responded.

Nitya nodded. Reaching into her purse, she pulled a card and handed it to Chirag. "Thank you for all your help. If you think of anything else, please call me," she said, pointing to the card. His face fell when Chirag read the card and realised where she worked. Nitya shot him a reassuring smile and sauntered out of the restaurant.

***

Swati's cheery demeanour struck Nitya as she whipped out a file and placed it on the coffee table. Getting out of the Delhi office and escaping all the uncertainty around the buyout had probably helped. Nitya had already relayed what she'd learned from Chirag at the lodge earlier that day. Sitting back, she started reading the papers that Swati had put together on Arvind Kapoor's family and business ventures.

"Do you believe there's a connection, ma'am, between Dinesh's disappearance and Arvind's death?"

"I don't know, but it's quite a coincidence. I mean, there is no obvious connection. But ..."

"What is it, ma'am?"

"We're missing something, and it's nagging at the back of my mind," Nitya muttered. Glancing up from the files, she noticed Swati fidgeting with her pen. "What's bothering you?"

"Maybe you shouldn't have told Chirag you're from the press. Now, he might warn the folks at the showroom that a reporter will be showing up to ask questions about Dinesh," Swati said.

"I understand, but that might work in our favour." She offered a confident smile and went back to reading Swati's notes.

"How?" she demanded.

"You will see," Nitya spoke without lifting her eyes from the document. "So, Arvind Kapoor co-owns another hotel?"

"Yes, ma'am, he and two other partners. That hotel is further up—north of his other property. Some place called Versova Beach. I'm unfamiliar with this city, but I marked it on a map." Swati reached into her bag and unfolded a big map of Bombay and its outskirts, spreading it on the table. The map bore four bright orange dots. "These are the two hotels," Swati continued, pointing to the ones near the coast. "This is his showroom," she added, pointing to the address in Andheri.

"And this one?" Nitya asked, pointing to the final dot.

"This is where he lives—I mean, where he lived," Swati replied, circling the fourth dot with her fingertip.

"Good work, Swati. I am impressed with everything you've managed to gather so far. Now, about the partners—"

"I couldn't," blurted Swati. "I mean, I tried calling them at their homes and businesses, but I couldn't contact them. I do have their names and addresses." She glanced up. "Oh, there is also another land holding, or some real estate, that they own in Delhi. But I don't know much yet. I'll keep digging."

"That's all right. You've done fantastic work given the short timeframe," Nitya said proudly.

"Thank you, ma'am. Where are we headed after this? The showroom?"

"No," Nitya replied, pausing to finish reading the file. "Our next visit is to the police station that's investigating Arvind Kapoor's death. Let's see if they tell us anything beyond matter is under investigation."

"Yes, that is what they normally say," Swati acknowledged with a sigh.

"Still, we must follow up and see if we can pry anything from them. Then, we head to the showroom where Dinesh worked." Looking her assistant over, she added, "You must be tired after your journey. Did you manage to get some sleep on the train?"

"I am fine," Swati responded in a brighter tone, a big smile stretching across her face. "I am just happy to be out and about instead of holed up in my cubicle, ma'am."

"But there is something on your mind? And before you tell

me, please, let's not discuss the merger and our office issues," Nitya stated, raising a palm in a warning.

"It's not that, ma'am." Swati shook her head.

"Then what is it?"

She paused, her eyebrows scrunched in thought. "What's drawing you to this case? Sure, there are unanswered questions about Dinesh's absence from work and a possible murder, but still."

"Do you recall the police raids on the warehouses in Delhi?"

"Yes," Swati said, her brow wrinkled. "What does that have to do with any of this?"

"And you're aware that the raids didn't yield much," Nitya continued.

Swati nodded. "You said there could be a mole at the station. But Dinesh didn't work for the police, as far as we know." Swati looked down at the table before locking eyes with Nitya again. "Oh, so you think ..."

"Maybe, just maybe, the warehouse where Dinesh worked was one of those targets. And perhaps he got mixed up with something he shouldn't have. I can't be certain, but I think we need to dig more," Nitya said.

A silence hung between them before Swati said, "Still, I see no connection to Arvind Kapoor."

"True. There isn't one at this point, apart from the fact that Dinesh worked in two of his establishments here in Bombay." Shifting her weight to get up, she caught Swati's gaze. "Shall we?"

Once outside, they hailed a taxi to drive them to the police station in Andheri. They arrived quickly, and Nitya couldn't hide her shock. The station was a mess. Reporters, photographers, and other interested parties were jostling to get through the main door. Some constables struggled to keep them out while simultaneously erecting barricades near the entrance.

"This is a lost cause," Swati said, pointing to the crowd clamouring at the station's entrance.

Nitya approached the throng and tapped the shoulder of someone who looked like a fellow journalist. She asked him what the commotion was about, and he informed her that it was Arvind Kapoor's murder. The police were not divulging any information. Turning back around, she shuffled over to Swati, standing on a street corner, far from the crowd.

"You're right. We aren't getting anywhere today with all this. But at least we know the police think it's a murder, not suicide," Nitya mused.

"So, we come back here tomorrow?" asked Swati.

"Yes, when it's less crazy. We're here for the whole week, and in any case, I don't expect the police to tell these folks anything. I'm sure we will read their official announcement in tomorrow's paper."

"To the showroom, then?"

"Yes, it's a short walk," Nitya said, gesturing toward the next crossing.

"A brisk stroll will do us some good," Swati nodded as they started down the sidewalk. When they lingered at a stoplight, Swati turned to Nitya. "Arvind Kapoor must have been a well-known figure, judging by how many reporters showed up at the police station."

"True, and from what we saw, his death will be quite a story," Nitya agreed. Within minutes, they were standing in front of a sprawling showroom on the ground floor of a large residential building.

Though the police had departed, much of the showroom was still cordoned off with police tape. Nitya looked around and spotted a café across from the building, where a host of uniformed employees from the showroom milled around. She assumed they weren't allowed back inside until the police completed their work. When she caught Swati's attention, she pointed to the café. Soon, Nitya and Swati were seated on an extended bench across from showroom workers who spoke in hushed tones. From the bits and pieces she could glean, Nitya gathered that most of the workers had already been questioned and were now waiting for their manager to come and speak to them.

After ordering some coffee, Nitya looked around. The other patrons in the café, those who didn't work in the showroom, were downing their beverages quickly and leaving. After a few moments, an elderly gentleman showed up to speak with the showroom workers. He announced that if they had already given their statements to the police, they could go home. He then warned them not to talk to the press or anyone else. As the man closed his brief speech, the workers started trickling out. Nitya noticed Swati shifting her leg to get up and follow them, but Nitya touched her arm, motioning for her to stay put. Once the workers left, the old man sat down, took out a handkerchief, and wiped away the beaded sweat on his brow.

Nitya got up, scooted her chair closer to him, and handed him her card. He glanced at it. Before he could say anything, Nitya babbled. "I know, I know, I just heard. 'Don't talk to reporters' and all that. You probably got word from Chirag, too, that I would also show up and ask questions," Nitya said.

"Honestly, ma'am, it's been quite a day. I don't feel like talking," the manager responded, averting his eyes.

"I understand, sir. But I am not here to talk about Mr Kapoor. You see, one of your ex-colleagues who worked in the showroom is missing," Nitya said softly.

"I'm aware. Chirag told me that you were asking questions about Dinesh at the hotel," he said.

"He must have also mentioned that I went to the police to get more details on his whereabouts. Perhaps they can do both at the same time," Nitya continued.

"What do you mean, 'both at the same time'?" the manager asked puzzledly.

"Well, they have already taken statements regarding Mr Kapoor. Perhaps they can now start looking into Dinesh Nath. I can request the investigating officer to summon your employees to the police station one by one," Nitya added.

"Is that needed? Most of these employees are new. Only a few old-timers were working during the time Dinesh was employed," the manager pleaded.

"Well, that's for the police to decide." Nitya gave him a curt smile. "I am sure they'd be eager to talk to everyone and get all the workers' accounts firsthand."

The old man groaned. "That means they won't be getting back to work, and this whole debacle will drag on for much longer," he huffed.

"Unless," Nitya said, tilting her head slightly toward Swati and then the manager.

"Unless what?" he demanded.

"You tell me something about Dinesh Nath that helps me find him. Then, I can tell the police that we're still looking into it, and I'll see if I can convince them to hold off on questioning the employees until we follow up on any leads you give us," Nitya suggested. She looked at Swati, who couldn't hold back a smile.

"I don't feel like talking to the press right now. In light of what has happened, I'm not even sure I should. And God only knows what you will print in the papers tomorrow," the man grumbled.

"Nothing, I promise you. Our conversation stays between us, off the record. You can deny it ever took place if it comes to that. In any case, there is nothing to report right now except that Mr Kapoor has died. How that happened is for the police to decide. I want to know where Dinesh Nath might have gone," Nitya said. The man shifted his gaze from her to Swati, who gave him an encouraging nod.

The manager drew a sigh. "All right, what do you want to know?"

"At the hotel, Chirag told us that Dinesh had left suddenly and had started working there. Do you know why? Was it Mr Kapoor's idea?"

"No. Mr Kapoor wasn't happy about him working in the showroom at all. I asked him once, but he seemed to suggest that he didn't have a choice in the matter," the manager replied.

"No choice? Mr Kapoor owned both the lodge and the showroom. That makes no sense." As Nitya spoke, she noticed Swati had brought out her notepad and started scribbling.

"I have no idea," the manager replied.

"How long did he work here?"

"Six months."

"And then he left of his own accord, or was he let go?" Nitya continued.

"He wasn't let go. I spoke to Dinesh briefly when he handed in his resignation. He mentioned that he was leaving because his wife had found a job in Delhi," the manager replied, his eyes darting away.

"But you think there was more to it, don't you?" Nitya pressed.

"Yes, although I don't know what that could have been. I know he had befriended a fellow after joining the showroom. Before you ask, it's not someone I know or an employee here.

During my last conversation with Dinesh, he told me that this person had made his life miserable, and he couldn't continue living in Bombay any more."

"Miserable? How?" Nitya asked.

"Unfortunately, he didn't share that with any of us. You can ask the other long-time employees, but he wasn't close to any of them. He kept his head down and did the work. I am the one he confided in the most," the manager claimed.

"This person that he befriended, you never saw him? He never came to the showroom?"

"No. Dinesh didn't give me his name either," the manager replied forcefully.

"Was he known to Mr Kapoor?"

"Maybe, but I wouldn't know. Mr Kapoor wasn't the type of boss who mingled with his employees. He was an old-school, no-nonsense business owner. He wasn't particularly friendly or social with anyone," the manager said, glancing around the coffee shop.

"Did Dinesh ever call you from Delhi?" Nitya went on.

"No. That was the last we heard of him until you showed up," the manager replied, shaking his head.

"What about his wife and daughter?"

"What about them?" the old man asked, furrowing his brow.

"Did he ever talk about his family, show you their pictures, mention how he met his wife? Anything?"

"No, he wasn't very chatty," the manager said, then shuffled his feet. "Now, if you don't mind, I must get going. Are you done with your questions?"

"Just one more," Nitya said, "and I promise you, Mr ..." She faltered. "I am sorry I didn't catch your name."

"Rahul Tandon," the manager replied.

"Right, Mr Tandon," Nitya continued, "what exactly did

Dinesh do in your showroom? What was his role?"

"Loading and unloading appliances, mostly the large air coolers. Essentially, he made sure they were packed properly before being shipped. And he guaranteed they were unloaded and displayed correctly in the showroom once they arrived," Rahul said quickly. "He wasn't involved in selling or interaction with customers."

"Well, those were all the questions I had," Nitya said with a smile, pointing to the business card he still clutched in one hand. "In case you think of anything else." With that, she glanced at Swati to check whether she wanted to ask anything.

"Sir," Swati said as Rahul got up to leave. He turned around. "Do you also deal with Mr Kapoor's business in Delhi?"

"No, I only manage the showroom here. I'm aware he had a minor stake in a business in Delhi. I think it's some land or property. All I know is his other partners were involved in managing that. One of them is from Delhi, or so I recall from what he told me," Rahul said in a rush.

"Thank you, sir," Swati replied. With that, Rahul spun around and fled the café in a hurry.

Nitya turned back to Swati. "Good question. I hadn't thought of that."

"What now, ma'am?"

"Next order of business—visit this other hotel in Versova Beach that Mr Kapoor co-owned and see if we can find out more about this elusive friend that prompted Dinesh and his family to leave Bombay."

Swati nodded in agreement. "We also need to get more info on these partners."

"Yes, that's important," Nitya said before flitting her eyes to the showroom across the street. "It's getting late, and I need to make some calls. Let's head back to the guesthouse for now. Then, you can follow up on Mr Kapoor's partners. I doubt they'll be keen to speak with us, but if you can locate their addresses in Bombay, we can visit them tomorrow after finishing with Versova in the morning."

"If you want, ma'am, I can head to Versova now and meet you back at the hotel later tonight to let you know what I find," Swati suggested.

Nitya grinned. "I like your enthusiasm. But there may be something sinister going on here. I don't want you doing this on your own. Let's solve this case together, shall we?"

"Sure, ma'am," Swati replied. After leaving the café, they hailed a taxi to return to their hotel.

***

Morning light streamed from the window of her room. Nitya yawned, deciding to get up early and take advantage of the warm weather. After getting dressed, she went for a run along Marine Drive. When she returned, still catching her breath, she spotted Swati pacing up and down the lobby. She ran up to Nitya as soon as she crossed the main entrance.

"What's going on?" Nitya asked through heaving breaths.

"Where were you? I have been trying to reach you in your room for the last hour, and then I tried the restaurant," Swati blurted.

"It's all right. I'm here now. What's the urgency?"

"We have been ordered back to Delhi immediately," Swati cried. "I got a call from Mr Kumar's secretary. He tried to reach you first, but when he couldn't, he called me. He said that we are to return to Delhi without delay," she continued, wringing her hands.

"All right, let's calm down. I will talk to him and then decide what to do. Let's meet back here in an hour for breakfast. If it's urgent, we will take the earliest train possible. But if not, I'd prefer we carry on here." Nitya touched Swati's arm gently to calm her.

Nitya's call with her new boss, Lalit Kumar, didn't go as expected. Lalit refused to elaborate on why they were being summoned back to Delhi, which made for a stressful journey to the train station as Swati kept pestering Nitya for answers she didn't have. She tried to allay her assistant's fears but to no avail. When they finally sat on the Rajdhani Express, Swati surveyed the train car and then turned to Nitya.

"That's strange," Swati remarked.

"What's that?"

"Oh, I could have sworn I saw the same gentleman on the train from Delhi and then again yesterday," Swati noted.

"What do you mean?" Nitya leaned forward, curious.

"That tall gentleman in the pale blue shirt, three rows behind us on the other side," Swati said, jerking her head slightly without looking back. "Maybe he is a fellow reporter."

Nitya waited till the train started moving. When it had left the station and picked up speed, she glanced at the man Swati was referring to. She couldn't see his face as he was reading a newspaper. "Are you sure?" Nitya whispered, her fingers grazing Swati's arm.

"Sorry?"

"This man," Nitya said, stopping Swati from looking back again. "Please, try to remember," she went on.

"I am not certain, ma'am. But I could have sworn I saw him outside Mr Kapoor's showroom yesterday," Swati stammered.

The hairs on Nitya's arms prickled as her mind reeled with questions. *Is someone following us? Someone who knows that Swati and I are in Bombay, and which story we're working on?* Nitya tried to calm herself. They had a long journey ahead. She would have plenty of time to walk back and forth a few times to get a good look at the mysterious passenger.

***

When they reached Delhi, Nitya rushed to her boss' office and instructed Swati to continue working on the story. As she approached, she was surprised to see the paper's owners through the large glass partition. She stepped back and waited. Once the Thapar brothers left, Lalit's secretary ushered her into the office. After they exchanged pleasantries, Lalit picked up the phone, asking his secretary to hold his calls for the next fifteen minutes.

"Now then, Nitya. What's happening with the new story that you've taken up?"

The question left Nitya stunned. Her boss was not a micromanager, and he rarely asked any of his reporters for updates unless it was an important story or they needed something from him. "I'm not quite sure, sir. There are still a lot of unanswered questions," Nitya responded.

"Tell me, why are you so adamant about this story?" Lalit snapped, his frankness surprising Nitya. Although he was always formal, he was usually much less confrontational.

"It's just that—"

"Never mind," Lalit grumbled, cutting her off. "We can discuss that later. You do realise that we are now part of a different organisation."

"I understand, sir," Nitya said, not wanting to argue further. At that, Lalit seemed to ease up. She sat back, waiting for him to explain why they had been summoned back to Delhi before engaging further.

"Well, something more important has come up. And it takes priority over what you and Swati are working on," Lalit said, reaching for a file on his large desk and handing it to Nitya. He continued while Nitya started leafing through the pages. "The file contains all the details of the new art building planned for Delhi University's north campus. Rumours are floating around concerning irregularities in the tendering process and how the contract was finally awarded."

Nitya scanned the file and then locked eyes with Lalit. "We were called back for this?" She jabbed a finger at the file.

"Yes, this is important. Crores of rupees, public money, are being spent on this, and our readers have a right to know whether this project is being carried out with due diligence and without corruption," Lalit responded, holding his chin high.

"Why me? My team normally doesn't deal with stories like this," Nitya asserted.

"True, but I contacted everyone, and they are all busy with other high-profile stories. So, I figured I'd hand it to you. This is an important story, and it requires every bit of your team's focus and, needless to say, your investigative acumen. And before you ask, yes. This takes precedence over the disappearance of some fellow we know little about—or even whether he is missing," Lalit shot back.

Nitya blinked back, struggling to hide her surprise. She hadn't mentioned Dinesh's disappearance to anyone except Swati. It was clear that Lalit knew more than he was letting on. But she wasn't willing to give up just yet.

"We can work on both stories. I'll free up some of the others on my team to prioritise this," Nitya said.

"No," Lalit growled, his tone startling Nitya. She leaned forward and, once again, fished for more details.

"Is this coming from you or someone else?"

"Why do you ask?" Lalit demanded.

"It seems this story has more to do with the Thapars losing the contract than anything else. Is that why they stopped by?" Nitya continued.

Lalit refused to look her in the eye. Getting up, he paced toward the door and turned around. "We all work for someone. And in our case, the owners of this paper are the Thapar Group. You're aware that, for the most part, they leave us alone to report on any story we want. You also know that they are far less meddlesome than other business houses that rule over prominent newspapers in this country."

"But—" Nitya began to protest, but Lalit raised a hand to stop her.

"Now, occasionally, they ask us to prioritise some stories over others. And they are well within their rights to do so. I don't know whether the assignment has arisen from their disappointment over losing the building contract or something else. They didn't say. But as long as we work for them, we must abide by their wishes. Again, for the last six months, even through all the turbulence of the merger, they have never once interfered in our day-to-day activities." With those words, Lalit opened his office door, signalling the meeting was over.

"Right, sir," Nitya mumbled. As she got up, her spirits sank. Before she left the room, Lalit turned to her.

"Please, keep me posted on how things are going," he said in a gentler tone.

"I will, sir." Nitya nodded, slipped out of the room, and trudged back to her desk.

On her way back, she spotted Swati in her cubicle. She was on the phone, engaged in an animated conversation. Though busy, the rest of her team greeted her and smiled as she walked past. Once she reached her desk, she started making phone calls regarding all the stories her team was following up on. It wasn't until late in the evening that she heard a knock on her office door. It was Swati, a well-worn notepad in hand. Nitya gestured to the chair across her desk.

"All good, ma'am?" Swati asked tentatively.

"Yes, nothing you need to worry about," Nitya replied, which brought a smile to Swati's face.

"So, why the rush to bring us back to Delhi?"

"Well, they want us to take on other stories and—you know—priorities always change. We'll talk about it later. Now, tell me what you have found out," Nitya said, leaning back in her chair.

"I've been on the phone all day, trying to contact the hotel in Versova Beach and then following up on the contacts they gave me. Although I haven't made headway on Dinesh's whereabouts, I may have found the link between Dinesh's workplace in Delhi and Arvind Kapoor." Swati opened her notepad and tore out a piece of paper, passing it to Nitya.

"What's the link?" Nitya asked. She left the paper on her desk, her eyes still focused on Swati.

"The warehouse where Dinesh worked is on the same co-owned property that the showroom manager mentioned. It's a storage facility on the outskirts of Delhi, near the Gurgaon border. Arvind Kapoor partly owns that facility." Swati struck her fist in her palm.

"What's stored at the warehouse? Appliances?" Nitya asked.

"Yes, mostly air coolers," Swati responded.

"Hmm, good. So, maybe this points to some nefarious

activity at the warehouse? Perhaps something Arvind Kapoor was involved in. We still don't know why he was killed, right?"

"Correct, ma'am. It's hard to infer much. But let's visit the warehouse tomorrow," Swati continued.

"We will." Nitya scratched her chin, hoping Swati couldn't sense the hesitation in her voice. "This is good, Swati. Anything on the partners?"

"No, ma'am. I am having difficulty getting through to them or digging up their details," Swati said.

"All right. Leave the partners to me."

"Thank you, ma'am," Swati said with a cheerful sigh. Nitya could sense the relief in her tone.

"What else?"

"One more thing. Do you recall that both the manager at the lodge, Chirag Seth, and the one at the showroom, Rahul Tandon, mentioned there was someone who had befriended Dinesh, who may have been responsible for his leaving Bombay with his family?"

"Yes, I remember."

"Well, after *many* phone calls to the various contacts the hotel in Versova gave me, I finally found him. He used to work at the Versova Beach hotel and moved to Delhi right after Dinesh," Swati said. "He is working in a hotel in this city."

"So, he is also in Delhi?"

"Not only that, I know where he works," Swati announced with a smirk. "His name is at the bottom of the page I handed you."

"Great work!" Nitya gushed. But when her eyes fell on the last line of the page, she froze, and time seemed to slow. Swati kept on talking, but Nitya couldn't hear a thing. Her gaze remained fixated on the name scrawled across the bottom of the sheet. Nalin Kohli. The same Nalin who was in a relationship with her sister, Kavita, and working at the same hotel.

Deception

Shankar didn't mind leaving the office, especially on brisk winter mornings like these when the streets of Delhi were sunny and bright. He had decided to start early and visit the warehouses before work. The row of gritty factories and looming warehouses that dotted the Delhi-Jaipur highway reminded him of the blue-collar towns scattered around his state. The only difference was that they were spaced out here, with groves of trees and lush vegetation filling the empty spaces between the properties. Given the rapid rise in industrial growth around the capital city, he wondered how long that would last.

After trying five warehouses, he finally found one where someone recognised Dinesh Nath. The guard at the gate pointed to the photograph and told Shankar that he worked there.

Once inside the gates, Shankar strolled up to the main building. It resembled a massive shed, with entry and exit points on all four sides. A row of lorries was parked beside a dirt road inside the compound. As he ambled up to the main entrance, where a small hut-shaped structure had been erected, he stopped, assuming this was the primary office.

The guard had already messaged the folks inside, notifying them that a policeman would ask questions about Dinesh. Shankar then talked to the employees individually, though most offered little or no information about Dinesh, except that he worked there and hadn't shown up for over a week. No one seemed too worried about his absence. Finally, after about an hour, a large white Ambassador rolled into the compound. The car door opened, and a man dressed in an impeccably white safari suit emerged. A few warehouse employees whispered something to him, pointing in Shankar's direction. The man marched up to Shankar and stretched out his hand.

"Namaste, Officer. My name is Vijay Salve. I am one of the owners of this warehouse. Is there something I can help you with?"

Shankar shook his hand and introduced himself. "I'm here to inquire about one of your employees, Dinesh Nath."

"Certainly. Perhaps we can head over to my office. We can chat more freely there," Vijay said, gesturing to an enclosed room inside the warehouse. The space was small yet tidy. Once seated across from each other, Vijay asked an attendant to prepare some tea and biscuits and then turned to Shankar. "I am afraid we haven't heard from Dinesh for some time. I have no idea where he might be."

"Maybe you can tell me where he lives, and I can visit his family. I'm assuming you have the address somewhere in your employee records," Shankar said.

"Of course, Officer Sen. We'll get that to you immediately. He lives in Old Delhi, I believe," Vijay babbled. He called his secretary over and instructed him to give Shankar the address of Dinesh's residence on file.

"Thank you." Shankar kept his eyes locked on Vijay to observe whether his expression changed. It didn't.

"Sorry, I am a bit confused, Officer. If his family didn't report him missing, who did?"

"Oh, one of his friends. He told us he was worried about Dinesh, so we started our inquiries," Shankar continued. Again, none of his statements seemed to faze Vijay, who maintained his pleasant disposition and guarded answers.

When the tray of tea and biscuits arrived, Vijay hailed one of the workers outside the door, asking him to bring the car around as he would be leaving soon. The worker disappeared on his errand, and Vijay turned back to Shankar. "Is there something else I can help you with?"

"Just a few things," Shankar began, sipping his cup. "We will need to talk to your other partners. Just routine stuff, checking off all our boxes, you know."

Vijay's pleasant smile fell, his expression growing more stoic. "You can talk to my brother, Vinay. I can give you his address, but if you wait thirty minutes or so, he should be arriving. I doubt he'll be able to tell you anything more about Dinesh, but you're welcome to ask."

"So, you two are the joint owners of this establishment?"

"We have a third partner, Arvind Kapoor, who resides in Bombay. However ..." Vijay's voice trailed off, and a sullen silence cloaked the room.

"What is it?" Shankar demanded.

"You see, he passed away yesterday." Vijay shifted his gaze to the side.

"Passed away? How?" Shankar pressed, leaning forward.

"We don't know. The police are still investigating," Vijay murmured.

"Why are the police involved? Wasn't it a natural death?"

"We don't know, Officer. Perhaps you can contact your counterparts in Bombay to get the details. What we heard was that it could have been either a suicide or a murder. There is no official word yet," Vijay said and then paused. Shankar didn't miss Vijay constantly stealing glances at the door. Shankar changed the topic, bringing the focus back to his missing person.

"What exactly did Dinesh do here?"

"It's a warehouse. He helped store, pack, unpack, and transport goods. That's all anyone ever does in a warehouse," scoffed Vijay, visibly unimpressed with the question.

"Really? I was under the impression he was a security guard."

Vijay's eyes widened, "Yes, well, the workers here wear many hats," he stammered.

"I understand, Vijay Ji," continued Shankar. "Can you think of any reason someone would want to hurt Dinesh? Were there any scuffles or arguments in the workplace that you are aware of?"

"Oh, yes. He had a heated argument with someone just outside the gates," Vijay said with a jolt. "I remember. I was leaving, and we couldn't get through the gate because they were blocking the entrance, yelling at one another. Something about money being owed that hadn't been paid."

"Money being owed to Dinesh, or Dinesh owing someone else money?"

"I haven't the slightest idea," huffed Vijay. "Do you think I get involved with every argument my employees have? I only recall this instance because it almost came to blows. Some other workers had to step in before things got worse."

"Can I speak to the other employee with whom he had an altercation?"

"That's the thing, Officer. The man in question doesn't work here. I'm not sure where he works or even what his name is. Only Dinesh seemed to know him. From what the workers told me afterwards, it seems the man worked at a hotel somewhere and knew Dinesh from his days in Bombay. It could be they were friends who had a falling out," Vijay said with a shrug.

"Right. Vijay Ji, I will follow your suggestion and wait for your brother here. Until he arrives, do you mind if I take a quick look around and perhaps talk to some of the other workers to see if they can shed light on this?" Shankar asked. "I can always come back with some colleagues and run this more formally, or I could ask your employees to stop by the station."

Shankar sensed Vijay's hesitation. "No, that's all right. Please, go ahead. Though I am hoping this is not a search or anything. I'd expect a proper warrant for that. I doubt anyone else can help you beyond what I've just told you."

"I understand. But I'll still chat with them in case they recall something pointing to Dinesh's whereabouts. That's all I am currently worried about," Shankar said.

Vijay sighed. "Fine. Please do what you please, but I will ask my manager to accompany you at all times. I assume that's not going to be a problem."

"None whatsoever," Shankar said with a quick nod. Their conversation was interrupted when a worker arrived, handing Shankar a paper that bore Dinesh's address.

Vijay dipped his head to Shankar, got up, and left the room. He hadn't even touched his tea or biscuits. Once Vijay's Ambassador rolled out of the compound, Shankar spent the next hour and a half questioning employees under the watchful eye of the warehouse manager. Vijay's brother, Vinay, showed up shortly after, and Shankar went through the same line of questioning. Vinay seemed even more guarded than his brother, and Shankar noted that he spent much less time at the warehouse and wasn't particularly interested in the business.

After finishing all the interviews, Shankar's shoulders sagged with exhaustion. But before heading out, he took one last look at the storage area. His eyes roved the gaping room, noticing the big lights hanging from the high ceilings and large portable fans around the space. Some mattresses and pillows were piled on the floor in one corner, and on the other side, he glimpsed a large water cooler and two big refrigerators. A pair of racks held clothes of various sizes. There were no goods in the warehouse at this time. The workers had mentioned waiting for a shipment from Shimla in a few days.

Shankar took down the shipment details and then ambled toward the main gates to exit the compound. But something caught his eye. A few lorries were parked on one side of the gate. After scribbling down some details, he walked up to where the drivers were resting and spoke to them briefly before leaving the campus. Shankar nodded at the guards and then crossed the street to his Jeep. Slowing down, he noticed a white Ambassador parked behind his vehicle, alongside a familiar face that brought a smile to his lips.

"Well, well, well. If it isn't the handsome Mr Shankar Sen," a friendly voice rang out.

"Nitya! What on earth are you doing here?" Shankar rushed up to her and gave her a big hug.

As they broke apart, Nitya gestured to the young woman beside her. "This is Swati," she said, angling toward her. Shankar gave her a nod, which she returned. Then, Shankar brought his attention back to Nitya.

"It's so nice to see you," he said. "We know each other well enough to meet somewhere more decent. Not outside a warehouse."

"I agree. We are in the same city, and it's unforgivable that we don't get together more often. I meant to call you," Nitya said. Shankar noticed that her demeanour grew more serious, and her smile fell. She and Swati shared a look that was heavy and meaningful.

"Is everything all right?" Shankar asked.

"Oh, yes," Nitya said, plastering another smile and touching

Shankar's arm instinctively. "But I do need some advice on a personal matter. Maybe we can meet at the Coffee House in Connaught Place tonight?"

"Personal matter, hmm? Well, in that case, it shouldn't be a problem," Shankar said with a grin, making Nitya laugh. "Sure, what time?"

"Let's say 9 p.m."

"Sounds good," Shankar said.

"Anyway, what brings you here?" Nitya motioned to the warehouse behind him. Shankar responded with a smirk. Before he could answer, Nitya continued. "I know, I know. 'We can't comment on an active investigation,' blah, blah, blah." She shook her head, and they both chuckled.

"I must be heading off, Nitya. I'm already late for work, but let's talk later tonight. I want to hear everything happening with you since that pesky acquisition." Shankar hugged Nitya again and smiled at Swati, who seemed puzzled by the exchange.

***

Back at the station, Shankar looked around for Ashok, but he wasn't in yet. Ignoring a prick of irritation, he shuffled to his desk and rifled through the messages left there. They were from his boss, asking Shankar to meet him right away. He ignored the request and instead called the Andheri Police Station in Bombay. After speaking with the officer investigating Arvind Kapoor's death, he placed calls to various locations in Bombay and Delhi. He looked at his watch. It was getting late. Stepping away from his desk, he asked another constable to check whether Ashok had arrived. But no one had seen him.

Meanwhile, Shankar decided to meet with Gagan Singh.

Usually, receiving multiple messages from his boss meant the higher-ups wanted something. Going by experience, that meant providing security cover for a politician or doing the rounds of the Home Ministry. This meant attending long meetings to deliver updates on their current activities. If he ignored the requests long enough, Shankar knew the duties would be passed on to one of his fellow officers, some of whom would be overjoyed to be thrust into the limelight.

Shankar settled into one of the complex folding chairs across from Gagan, who was on the phone. While he waited, Shankar glanced around the office. The room had a dark, foreboding look, and Shankar often wondered whether the décor and furniture were unfriendly by design. Gagan Singh, on the other hand, was an amiable character. He had climbed the ranks and prided himself as a boss who liked to keep everyone happy. He seldom looked stressed, which was uncommon for a man in his post, and the whole station knew that he rarely rocked the boat when it came to making unpleasant decisions. Putting down the receiver, Gagan glanced at the files on his desk, quickly closed them, and brought his eyes to Shankar.

"Ah, Sen. How goes the battle against the lowlifes in this city?"

Shankar smiled. *At least he's in a good mood.* "I have no idea, sir."

"Ha! That's what I like about you. A sense of humour and honesty," Gagan said with a bellowing laugh.

"I got your two messages. Sorry, I was away working a strange case," Shankar said, catching the slightest change in Gagan's expression.

"I know very well what's on your plate. This ghastly narcotics business," Gagan started. "Is there something new that has come your way?"

"Well, it's too early to say, but I reckon we are dealing with a missing person, one who may be involved in questionable activities," Shankar said thoughtfully.

"Who is missing?"

"A guard from the library who also works at a warehouse on the Delhi-Haryana border," Shankar said.

"Hmm. And why is this of interest to us? Is it a warehouse we raided?" Gagan asked, folding his hands over his chest.

"No, sir," Shankar replied.

"Then what's this nefarious activity you suspect?"

"Well, something was a bit off at the warehouse," Shankar responded, stroking his chin.

"How so?"

"I noticed quite a few lorries, though the warehouse was empty. The owners told me they weren't expecting any new supplies for days. But when I spoke to the lorry drivers, they claimed otherwise," Shankar said.

Gagan hummed in thought. "Well, perhaps they don't know. Change of plans, maybe?"

"It's possible, sir," Shankar said slowly. "But the lorries ..."

"What about them?"

Before Shankar could continue, the phone started ringing. Gagan picked up the receiver and spoke with the Home Minister about another case. Shankar motioned to ask whether Gagan wanted him to leave, but Gagan raised his hand, requesting him to stay put as he carried on his animated discussion.

"Unbelievable," Gagan sighed after hanging up. "What do these guys expect? They want us to solve anything and everything the minute it happens," Gagan huffed.

"Is there something I can help with, sir?"

"Oh, no. Thank you, Shankar," Gagan said before quickly

examining an open file on his desk. "Where were we? Ah, yes. The missing guard and the warehouse," he continued before Shankar could reply. "Is there anything concrete to warrant one of my best officers' valuable time?"

"Mostly a hunch, sir. But the more we dig into this person's identity, the stranger the trail gets," Shankar responded.

"Right. My concern is whether this should take priority over the drug case. Do you think they are connected?" Gagan leaned forward, propping his elbows on his desk.

Shankar thought for a moment. He worried that Gagan might ask him to drop Dinesh's case altogether and hand him something else to work on. Since he first started looking into the disappearance, Shankar wasn't even sure whether a missing person's report had been filed—by Bharat or anyone else. If not, that gave him even less of a reason to continue. He fixed his eyes on Gagan, who was still awaiting an answer.

"No, sir, it doesn't take precedence. And there is one more thing you ought to know since we are on this topic."

Gagan tilted his head. "What's that?"

"I spoke to two of the three warehouse owners earlier today. The third partner, who's from Bombay, was found dead. I spoke to the investigating officer in Bombay, and it looks like he's been murdered," Shankar said.

"Wow! Too big of a coincidence, you think?"

"That's right, sir," Shankar agreed.

Gagan once again flitted his gaze to the file in front of him. He closed it and turned to Shankar. "What's next? I mean, what do you plan to do with all this?"

"I was actually about to come and discuss that with you, sir. While at the warehouse, I noticed a few documents suggesting the facility is scheduled to receive a shipment of appliances from Shimla."

"Shimla?" quizzed Gagan.

"Yes, sir. My question is whether I have permission to go there and find out, at the source, what's being shipped. Perhaps I can uncover what's going on," Shankar said, then paused.

Gagan leaned back into his chair, and Shankar noted that his expression became more stoic. After a long minute, his boss broke the pregnant pause. "All right, if you think visiting Shimla is crucial for this case, go for it. Please keep me informed of your progress."

Shankar's response was interrupted when the phone on Gagan's desk again rang. Before Gagan could pick it up, Shankar quickly asked, "I believe you wanted to talk to me about something?"

"What?" Gagan gave him a puzzled look as he picked up the receiver.

Shankar lowered his voice. "The messages, sir, on my desk this morning."

Gagan put his hand over the mouthpiece. "Oh, don't worry about it. We will talk when you get back. Have a safe trip."

With that, he turned his attention to his phone call—Shankar's cue to leave. He smiled, nodded, and got up from his chair. As he left the room, Gagan's booming voice echoed behind him. His boss was having a heated conversation with one of his peers in another station about a politician's relative who had been taken into custody.

While trudging back to his office, Shankar couldn't help but ponder Gagan's strange behaviour with that file on his desk. It almost seemed he wanted to talk to Shankar about it but then decided against it. What bothered him more was that Gagan didn't share why he had left those urgent messages for Shankar to meet with him as soon as he reached the station.

***

The Coffee House in Connaught Place was packed with locals and tourists enjoying stiff drinks and warm beverages on a Delhi winter's night. The dense fog made the surroundings look colder than they were. Shankar arrived first and requested a booth at the restaurant's end in a secluded corner. He was lucky that some patrons were leaving. He hustled to the booth, settled in, and brought out a newspaper to read while waiting for Nitya. How many years had it been, he wondered? They'd first met during their days in Callipur, where he was first posted, and their friendship had kindled through common cases and news stories.

They last met during Diwali, when they ran into each other at a gala in a New Delhi hotel. Shankar enjoyed Nitya's company. She was one of the few people he could talk to, frankly. Though she was a journalist, Nitya was fair. She knew where to draw the line and never betrayed his confidence if they discussed something off the record.

As she walked in, Shankar waved her over. She drew the gazes of other patrons as she sauntered right past them in her blue sari. After squeezing Shankar in a long embrace, she sat down with a beaming smile. Shankar folded his newspaper, put it away, and called for the waiter. They ordered some drinks, along with kebabs, dal, and naan. Soon, they were immersed in conversation, sharing memories from their past. When the food arrived, Nitya finally voiced what was on her mind, explaining that she needed Shankar's help before he could ask.

"Now, remember that this is strictly off the record," she began. As she launched into her story, Shankar patiently heard everything she'd learned in Bombay and Delhi concerning Dinesh Nath. Before Shankar could offer his opinion, the waiter came by with their order. He carefully laid out the plates and served them their drinks. Shankar noted the slight pull of Nitya's mouth, the concern brewing behind her eyes. She had become more serious since she first arrived. When the waiter left, they dug into their food, and after a few helpings, Nitya once again spoke first.

"Shankar, I am worried sick about Kavita. I don't know to what extent Nalin is caught up in all this."

"Presumably, you have spoken to your sister already?" Shankar asked, putting his fork down.

"I have, but as you can imagine, she is confused. She doesn't know what to make of it. I mean, what if he has nothing to do with all this? It could be that Dinesh is involved in these illegal activities, and Nalin just got involved with the wrong person," Nitya said quickly.

Shankar kept silent, his eyes falling to the table. "Tell me, does Kavita believe that Nalin might be capable of duping another man or causing him harm?"

"I don't know. Until now, she was sure he was a decent fellow, but love clouds one's judgment. When I first told her all this, she became defensive and didn't want to hear anything against Nalin. But now ..." She shifted her gaze to the other end of the restaurant.

"What?" asked Shankar.

"Now, she is not so sure." With a sigh, she turned her attention back to Shankar.

"Is that because you wore her down with your pestering, or did something else happen?" Shankar raised his eyebrows.

"Well, Kavita told Nalin about my trip to Bombay. I haven't shared all the details with her, but I did mention the untimely death of Arvind Kapoor and that we were looking into the story. After she mentioned this to Nalin in passing, his behaviour changed. He became more distant and aloof. In any case, things have calmed down. Nalin had to go to Bombay and will be there for a few days now, so I don't have to worry about Kavita being with him. But I do fear that he may indeed be part of a gang and that he was involved in the disappearance of Dinesh Nath. I also worry what he might do to my sister," Nitya said, her tone sullen and pensive.

"What reason did Nalin give Kavita for his trip to Bombay?"

"What do you mean?" Nitya scrunched her eyebrows as she picked up her fork and stabbed into a juicy kebab.

"I mean, Kavita and Nalin work together. She would know if this was a business trip or something more personal, right?"

"Ah, yes. He told her it was personal but didn't share more details. He does have family in Bombay," Nitya said, taking another bite.

"Right." As he thought it all over, he bit into his naan, and they focused on their meals. Halfway through his plate, Shankar paused and glanced at Nitya. "Is there anything else you would like to add?"

"Not about Kavita or Nalin. But I have a question, and I understand if you can't answer it. You were also in the warehouse earlier today because of Dinesh Nath. He works there—or at least worked there—and his case has landed on your desk, right?" Nitya drilled him with a stare.

Shankar smiled. "I can't discuss the investigation with the press, but since we're here as friends and off the record, I am looking into Dinesh's disappearance."

"And I am guessing you are now heading to Shimla to check on the source of the incoming shipment of appliances?" Nitya continued.

His eyes widened. "Wow, I am impressed. I went there as a police officer, and it took some convincing to get them to open up. I'd have thought they would steer clear of journalists. Yet you found out. Good show, Nitya," Shankar said, and they both laughed.

"Well, it's not just me. Swati, my colleague whom you met, is a pesky reporter and keeps digging no matter what obstacles are thrown her way," Nitya said.

"Much like her boss, I'd imagine," Shankar teased, picking up his fork.

"Careful, mister," Nitya joked, but her smile faded. "Shankar, there is something else, and I don't know what to make of it." Her voice became more solemn.

"What is it?"

"Something that Swati told me. Let me first say that it could be her vivid imagination, and it may amount to nothing, but still..."

"How about you tell me, and maybe I can help?" Shankar suggested.

She breathed deeply. "Swati joined me in Bombay a few days after I left Delhi. On our journey back, she said she spotted a gentleman she'd seen on her trip from Delhi, then again at a location we stopped at to investigate, and then a third time on the train back."

"And did you see this gentleman as well?" Shankar asked.

"On the way back, yes. And before you ask, I had never seen him before, and there is nothing to suggest that anything suspicious is going on. It could be pure chance. Still ..."

"Hmm, I know what you mean," Shankar sighed. "Have you or Swati seen him since your return to Delhi?"

"No," Nitya responded, "and that's why I am not sure there's anything to it."

"Right, and you both would recognise him if you saw him again?"

"Most certainly," Nitya confirmed. "In any case, I've asked Swati to use the company car on business and when driving to and from work. And, of course, to stay alert. There isn't much else I can do."

After a few moments, their conversation again drifted back to their past. As they finished their meal, Shankar reeled it back to the present.

"How are things with Professor Jai? I spoke to him briefly during Diwali at your place. He seems nice." Shankar could sense Nitya tensing up at his words.

"Yes, he is a nice man and a good friend. But we lead busy lives. Finding time for one another is a challenge. As you know, a journalist's job is not the typical nine-to-five, much like a policeman's," Nitya declared.

Shankar breathed a sigh and nodded. "Tell me about it. I hardly seem to finish one day before the next one's climbing all over me."

"How are things with Vikram and Rohini?"

"Vikram's growing up fast," Shankar responded with a smile. "He's settled into his school in Dehradun. I try to see him as often as possible, but it's not nearly enough if you ask me." Shankar shook his head.

"It must be hard." Nitya gave him a pitying smile before continuing in a hushed tone. "And Rohini?"

"I don't know. She seems happier in Dehradun. When she was here, she was lonely, missing her parents. And honestly, I couldn't spend much time with her. She tried her best, I think. But, you know," Shankar mumbled.

"Have you thought of moving to Dehradun? If there's an opening there?"

"Well, as you know, I am not from the state cadre. I'd have to get a special assignment or a role that requires me to be stationed there, and that's not easy. You're well aware of my past. I am still viewed as a bit of an outsider. Sure, a transfer to Dehradun might still happen, but it's unlikely," Shankar added. A silence stretched between them as they glanced at some patrons at the other tables who were getting up to leave.

"Coffee?" Nitya asked, turning to Shankar.

"Sure," Shankar replied. They hailed a waiter and ordered coffee with some rasgullas.

"What should I tell Kavita about Nalin, in your opinion? Should she stop seeing him? I don't even know if she'd agree," Nitya said, leaning forward.

"As you said, it's good he is in Bombay. Hopefully, that will give us both some time to investigate things further. To answer your question, it would be prudent for Kavita to keep her distance until all this is sorted out," Shankar affirmed.

Nitya nodded as the coffee and rasgullas arrived. After Shankar's response, Nitya became more serious and lost in thought. Then, she reached into her bag and brought a piece of paper. She placed it on the table and locked eyes with Shankar. "This is where I will be in Shimla tomorrow evening. The day after tomorrow, I'll head to the address that Swati uncovered in her research. I shouldn't be telling you all this, but I'm worried about Kavita, and I'm not sure how all this will end."

Shankar instinctively leaned forward, placing his hands on the table. "Don't worry, Nitya. I will do my best to get some answers as quickly as possible. Meanwhile, I do have a request."

"What's that?" Nitya cocked her head to the side.

"That you don't visit the location in Shimla alone," Shankar said.

"Why not?"

"We don't know what we'll find there. I'll be going there with help from the local station, so if you want—"

"Now, wait a minute! I need to keep working on this story, and ..." Nitya reined in her outburst when some patrons at the adjoining tables stopped to look at them. Nitya glanced in their direction, smiled, and then turned her attention back to Shankar.

"Please, let me finish," Shankar pleaded.

"I don't like where this is heading," Nitya grumbled, leaning back into her chair and crossing her arms.

"I know, but hear me out. I will be heading to that same address the day after tomorrow. You can follow us, and once we have scoped out the location, you're free to do what you want."

Nitya averted her gaze, her jaw tight. Shankar knew she didn't like him getting in her way. But he also knew she was worried about Kavita, which would entice her to accept his offer. She reached for her coffee cup, gripped it tightly, and took a sip, avoiding Shankar's gaze. Finally, she relented.

"Fine. I would normally never, *ever* agree to this. But this time, I will take you up on your offer. On one condition," Nitya stated.

Shankar released a breath of relief. "What's that?"

"Once you have ensured the location is safe, you and the other policemen will not prevent me from exploring the premises."

"Agreed," Shankar said with a smile.

"See? You are not the only one who can be difficult." Nitya winked, and they both laughed.

"Yes, I know," Shankar said with a nod.

"No, no, no." Nitya shook her head vigorously. "As a friend, you are supposed to say, 'No, Nitya. That's not true,' and then tell me wonderful things about myself to make me feel better."

"Ah, I will keep that in mind. But in my opinion, a true friend tells you what they think while letting you know that you are wonderful regardless," Shankar said with a hearty chuckle before biting into a plump rasgulla.

"You do have a way with words, mister. If you ever consider a career in writing, let me know," Nitya teased.

"Speaking of work, how is the new paper? *The Daily Citizen News* is a much bigger publication. It must be quite an adjustment."

"Yes, it's certainly bigger, but it's a different kind of paper with a different management style," Nitya said.

"Oh, do I hear a hint of discontentment?"

"I wouldn't go that far. Not just yet, at least. We are still going through the motions of the merger, and I'm willing to wait and see how things pan out once the dust settles. But for now, there's a lot of uncertainty. Not an easy place to be when you're managing a team of young reporters who are restless and looking for definitive answers," Nitya remarked.

"I can't say that I can relate." Shankar took a sip of his coffee. "But they have a wonderful journalist in their midst, and they'd be foolish not to see that."

"Ah, I haven't heard that kind of flattery. You should have led with that. Then, I might have been more receptive to your requests," Nitya said with a laugh.

"I'll keep that in mind for next time," Shankar agreed, nodding as their conversation veered into other topics. They were the last to leave the restaurant, and after Shankar walked Nitya to her car, he smiled to himself. He couldn't remember the last time he'd had such an enjoyable evening.

***

The next morning, Shankar found Ashok fidgeting with his pen outside his office. He ushered his constable inside, quickly scanned the files on his desk, and then turned to him.

"We're changing things up a bit, Ashok," Shankar started.

"Sir?"

"I need you to focus on something else," he continued.

Ashok's brows furrowed. "You mean we are not heading to Shimla?"

"I am, but I have something else in mind for you. It's time to do some old-fashioned police work," Shankar said with a smirk. "I need you to go through the archives and find everything you can on Arvind Kapoor, his two partners with whom he owns the Gurgaon warehouse and a Juhu hotel."

"Understood, sir."

Shankar gave him a pointed look. "Needless to say, this stays between us. Are we clear?"

"Yes, sir," Ashok responded. Glancing at the files on Shankar's desk, he asked, "What did Mr Gagan want?"

Shankar tilted his head. "Why do you ask?"

"This morning, when I ran into him in the canteen downstairs, I felt he wanted me to share what we were working on."

"That's not that surprising, is it?" Shankar asked.

"Sir, it is. He has never asked me about our cases. We have never even had a full conversation. Strangely, he is suddenly interested in what I'm doing."

"Perhaps not," mumbled Shankar, glancing at the door.

Ashok stared back, clearly confused. "Is there something I'm missing?"

Shankar sighed. He knew he could rely on Ashok, but his loyal aide could get caught up in the aftermath if things took a wrong turn. Then again, Ashok did have a right to know what was going on since he was actively involved in the investigation. Shankar paused and fixed his eyes on Ashok, who still looked puzzled. "Remember when we talked about a mole in our midst?"

"Yes, sir. Unfortunately, with all the leads I've been chasing regarding Dinesh, I haven't had time to focus on that," Ashok said. "You'd asked me to get you the phone records, but I haven't gotten around to it. I'm still not sure how running off the records of all outgoing calls from the switchboard will help. That's hundreds of numbers to sort through. It will take us forever to figure out who our colleagues were calling."

"I think I have a fair idea who the mole is—one of them, anyway. That's another thing. There is more than one person involved," Shankar said thoughtfully.

"Oh!" Ashok gasped. "We should nab him and interrogate him."

"No, no. At this point, I want to keep this on the down-low and maybe use him to point us in the right direction. If he thinks we suspect him, he'll bottle up. Do you understand?"

"Yes, sir, I get it," Ashok replied before staring blankly at the wall behind Shankar. "Are you going to tell me who it is? How did you find him?"

"When I met with Gagan Ji, he asked about the case. What I found surprising was that he also asked about your absence at the meeting," Shankar said.

"Oh my God. Mr Gagan Singh himself!" Ashok blurted, startling Shankar, who glanced at the door and then turned to Ashok.

Shankar held up his palms. "No, no, no. He is not the one. Or at least, I don't think he's involved in any way. But he seemed to know where you had been. And then, when I couldn't find you in the office yesterday morning, it confirmed my suspicions about who he's been getting the information from," Shankar said.

"What do you mean, sir? I haven't told anyone," Ashok declared.

"I know, but think about it. Who else knew that you were going around investigating Dinesh?"

"Just you and me, sir," Ashok affirmed.

"Really?" Shankar smirked, giving Ashok a moment to figure it out. "Did you drive to those places yourself, or ..."

"My driver, Ketan Lal! I don't believe it."

Shankar nodded. "He is the only other person who knew what you were up to."

Ashok cursed under his breath. "That scoundrel!"

"Careful, Ashok. We don't want to cause any waves. And remember, he must go about his business without knowing we're on to him. I have asked another trusted officer from a nearby police station to keep tabs on him. Ketan has been temporarily assigned to Mr Gagan's colleague, Mr Murthy, who is visiting from Chandigarh. The assignment was already planned, and I didn't want to mess with anything. If we insisted his duties be changed, he might get suspicious. For now, we keep an eye on Ketan to see if he leads us anywhere," Shankar said, letting Ashok absorb his words.

Ashok just kept staring at the wall. Then, his eyes snapped back to Shankar. "How did you know it was him? It could have been me as well."

Shankar smirked. "Yes, it could have. I had to be sure. Ketan was also looking for you yesterday, and he came by to ask me about you. I told him where you were. Then, when I spoke to Gagan Ji, he seemed to know already."

Ashok smiled. "And you tested me the same way?"

"I did," Shankar said with a grin. "I told you where I was

going, and when I spoke to Gagan Ji, he had no idea where I'd been. That confirmed it wasn't you," Shankar replied.

"Well played, sir," Ashok said, a glint of admiration in his eyes.

"I still need those phone records on my desk when I return from Shimla. The reason I called you concerns something that struck me while I was at the warehouse," Shankar said, leaning forward in his chair.

"What is it, sir?"

"Before I get to that, tell me. When we performed those raids, what did we use for transportation?"

"Our police vans, as well as some trucks, because we couldn't all fit into the vans," Ashok said with a puzzled look.

Shankar arched his eyebrows. "Where did those trucks come from?"

"A company that rents them out to our station at short notice, I believe," Ashok said. "I am sorry, sir, but I am still a little lost."

"Just stay with me for a bit, and you will know soon enough," Shankar said. Reaching into his pocket, he pulled out a scrap of paper and unfolded it. He placed the sheet on his desk. "These lorry companies are notified beforehand when we need their trucks, right?"

"Yes, usually a day or two in advance, and ..." His eyes bulged. "Oh my God! I think I know what you're getting at."

"Right. Each time our station orders lorries from these trucking companies, they know there will be a raid. They may not know where, but they surely know when," Shankar said, pausing to let his revelation sink in. Ashok's eyes glazed over, and Shankar sensed he was playing everything out in his head.

"Wow! How did you gain this information at the warehouse?"

"The lorries reminded me of the ones we use on our raids,"

Shankar responded. Then, he pointed to the paper. "I want you to find out whether these are registered to the same company from which our station rents lorries."

"Unbelievable," Ashok said, shaking his head. "To think, we may have more than one person tipping off these criminals right under our noses."

"I'd hoped it wouldn't come to all this," Shankar muttered. "Well, there's work to be done, and I have a long drive to Shimla."

"Right, sir. Good luck. I will keep you posted on what I find," Ashok said. With that, he got to his feet and took his leave. Shankar shifted his gaze to the last document on his pile and opened it. He had shared a lot with Ashok. But not everything.

***

The winter mist around Shimla made driving treacherous. On a clear day, the beautiful town nestled in the Himalayas was a feast for the eyes. Shankar's Jeep veered onto the winding road that climbed to their destination. As Shankar admired the mountain range, he momentarily forgot everything else. The frosty peaks reminded him of his childhood in Dehradun and Mussoorie.

They rolled along slowly, passing through a few police checkpoints that kept traffic flowing safely on the steep roads and ensured no roadblocks. Once in a while, Shankar would glance at the rearview and side mirrors to check that the police van was still following them. He had enlisted the support of a few constables from the local station. Behind the truck was the press car, an Ambassador in which Nitya was travelling with her driver.

Shankar had called her at her guesthouse the night before, arranging for her car to follow their convoy. Once they finally reached their destination, Shankar asked his driver to stop a few hundred meters outside the wooded compound. A long dirt road flanked by snow-capped vegetation snaked beyond the wooden gate that served as an entrance to a windowless concrete warehouse. There were no signs of vehicles or people anywhere. Shankar asked the convoy to wait near the gate while he approached the structure with a few constables.

A shroud of mist, the crunch of fresh snow under their boots, and the crisp smell of melt-off on the ground enveloped them as they trudged to the gate. Once they reached the warehouse, Shankar gestured for one of the constables to open the large door. They peeked inside, noticing that the lights on the high ceiling were still on. Shankar directed a few constables to survey the exterior while he stepped inside.

He spent the next half hour taking careful stock of the near-empty interior. There were two rooms in one corner, one with a phone. He picked up the receiver, but there was no dial tone. Hanging up, he spotted a large filing cabinet in the next room. Papers were strewn all over the room, and there were signs that people had eaten their meals on the floor. In the corner, a walk-in closet was filled with blankets and racks normally used for storing clothes. A few torn jackets and shredded shawls were clumsily hung.

After finishing his sweep, Shankar stepped outside and scrutinised the exterior for the next twenty minutes. He spoke briefly to the local constables who knew the area well. Satisfied there was no danger, he instructed a constable to bring Nitya in. Shankar ushered her into the warehouse and stood at the main door while she surveyed the space. Once she'd explored the whole warehouse, Shankar walked Nitya back to her car. But before climbing into the Ambassador, she turned to Shankar.

"They knew you were coming."

Shankar shrugged, peering back down the path they were on.

"Oh, come on, Shankar! It doesn't take a genius to figure out that whoever was here left in a hurry. Someone tipped them off," Nitya said.

Shankar sighed and then pivoted to face Nitya. She was right. There was no hiding that whatever was happening was more significant than they'd anticipated. A cloak of fog still hung in the air, and Shankar suppressed a shiver. Nitya opened her mouth to say something, then stopped when a constable approached to chat briefly with Shankar. Once he left, Shankar faced Nitya again.

"Off the record, Nitya, you may be right," Shankar said, scratching his neck as the idea took root.

"We both got played," Nitya mumbled.

"What do you mean?" Shankar kept his eyes locked on Nitya's.

"I was summoned back from Bombay to work on another story. When I approached my superiors to let them know I'd be travelling to Shimla for the story they didn't want me working on, I was surprised at how quickly they agreed. I'd expected an argument, but nothing. They just said yes. That should have been a red flag," Nitya said, her eyebrows drawn in thought.

"I am sorry, Nitya. I don't understand. Are you saying that your bosses didn't want you to pursue the story of Dinesh's disappearance and then agreed when you told them you'd be coming to Shimla to follow up on that same story?" Shankar asked, inching closer.

"Precisely. Now, why on earth would they agree, unless ...?"

"They expected you to find nothing here," Shankar said, finishing her sentence.

"Strange, isn't it? The only explanation I can think of is—" Nitya cut herself short. She looked at the warehouse and then at Shankar. "Are you thinking what I'm thinking?"

"Yes," Shankar muttered. "Time for us to go back to Delhi and find out what exactly is going on."

"This was a wasted trip," sighed Nitya.

"Not quite," Shankar remarked. "We both know that our superiors didn't want us to continue this investigation, yet there was no objection when we decided to come to Shimla. They knew we wouldn't find anything," Shankar said.

"They threw us off the trail. But what's the connection?"

"That's what we need to find out," Shankar said.

"Either way, we wasted precious time," Nitya huffed.

"That's one way of looking at it," Shankar said, unable to contain his smile.

"What? I don't find this funny, Shankar."

"Well, the Nitya I know will now relentlessly pursue this story until she uncovers the truth," Shankar said, and Nitya's expression lightened. She smiled and touched Shankar's arm.

"Aided by a police officer who happens to be a troublemaker?"

"Ha!" Shankar laughed. "It's good to see you haven't lost your sense of humour."

"I wish I were as relaxed as I sound," Nitya said. "I have to tread carefully now. Not only because of what's happening here and how it might be connected to my paper but also for Kavita's sake."

"Yes," Shankar said, his smile falling. "Caution would be prudent until we find out what exactly is going on here—and, more importantly, who we are dealing with."

"I am guessing you will be doing the same?" Nitya asked, an eyebrow arched.

"Oh no. Quite the opposite, actually," Shankar said, glancing at the police van behind his Jeep. "I am going back to Delhi to blow things wide open."

Library

Swati was quiet as she sat across Nitya's desk, listening to everything that had unfolded in Shimla.

"Do you have any questions?" Nitya asked once she finished her story.

"That officer we met at the warehouse in Gurgaon, who went to Shimla with you," Swati started.

"Shankar Sen. What about him?"

"Did he say anything of interest, ma'am?"

"Other than lamenting that he got played as well, no," Nitya responded. "And this stays between us. Something is going on here that I can't wrap my mind around. Not just yet," she continued. As she spoke, she noticed a mischievous glimmer in Swati's eyes.

"You seem friendly with him," she said, which made Nitya smile.

"He is a good friend," she replied. "I have known him for a long time. We were in Callipur together when he was investigating the murder of a mechanic. Then, we worked on another story a few years ago, following the unrest in Old Delhi. Remember, in our earlier paper, you worked on that as well as?"

"Oh, yes, of course. I remember the story about the riots," Swati nodded.

"Well, Shankar was the investigating officer in one of the Old Delhi police stations."

"He seems sharp. Not the kind of officer you normally see," Swati declared.

Nitya laughed. "No, he doesn't quite fit the stereotype that comes to mind when we think of policemen. Is there anything else? You can speak freely, you know."

"Just that he is a handsome fellow. I mean, don't you think?" Swati said in a hushed tone.

"And there it is," Nitya chuckled. "Yes, I suppose he is rather handsome."

"And you never ..."

"If you want to know, he is married, and we are good friends. Nothing more," Nitya said, still laughing.

"Oh, that's disappointing," mumbled Swati before joining Nitya's laughter.

"Aren't you the one getting married soon?"

"Yes, I know, but still," Swati teased.

"Can we get back to our story, please? We can talk about Shankar later if you are so interested," Nitya said.

"Fine," Swati sighed, glancing at her notepad. "Isn't it strange that both you and Shankar got played by your respective organisations? If I didn't know any better, I'd say there's a larger conspiracy at play here, with an insider in the police department."

"Oh, I am sure Shankar is well aware of that. He didn't say so explicitly, but I feel he made the same connection," Nitya stated.

"And this whole thing gets murkier with every step," Swati added.

Nitya dipped her head. "How about things here? Did you make progress on Arvind's business holdings?"

"I did," Swati replied, opening a large folder stuffed with papers. From the red numbers on each sheet, Nitya assumed they were arranged in a particular order.

"You can talk while I read through them," Nitya remarked.

"Sure, ma'am," Swati started. "Their holding here is the

warehouse we visited, where we saw some papers resembling invoices from trucking companies. I had taken down some details during our visit and started calling them individually."

"And?" Nitya waved her on, still reading the papers.

"I stumbled upon some addresses, where the trucks are coming from and where they are heading," Swati continued. "If you look at the first two sheets," she said, pointing to the sheaf of papers in Nitya's hand, "you will see that they are driving from the hotel in Versova Beach, Bombay, and heading to Jaisalmer in Rajasthan."

"That doesn't make sense."

"No, it doesn't. If they are transporting appliances, why would they be coming from a hotel to a Gurgaon warehouse and then heading to Jaisalmer?" Swati tapped her chin.

"Did you find out more about this address in Jaisalmer?"

"Yes, ma'am," Swati replied hurriedly, searching through her notes. "Here it is." She handed over a map with a handwritten note on a tiny dot near Jaisalmer.

"Am I seeing this right? It's at the western tip of town, nothing beyond it except the Thar Desert," Nitya said.

"And the border past that," Swati added, glancing at the wall behind Nitya.

Nitya leaned back in her chair, studying the map again. "So, they are smuggling something across the border."

"That's what it would seem." Swati nodded.

"What's the cover? The companies have to specify what they are transporting, right?"

"They do, ma'am. If you look at the description of the goods in the transport documents, you'll see they're mostly air coolers. That, I can understand. Jaisalmer is in the middle of a desert, one of the hottest places in India during the summer. But so many air coolers, so frequently—especially in winter—doesn't make sense," Swati said, shaking her head.

Nitya nodded gently. "What are they bringing back? Presumably, the trucks are not returning empty."

"Mostly clothes, blankets, and sheets. That bit is confusing, too. Unless new mills or factories have popped up recently, western Rajasthan isn't known for manufacturing textiles." Swati fixed her eyes on Nitya.

"Well, we did see some clothing racks in the warehouses in Gurgaon and Shimla. But you are right—they are probably hauling something else," Nitya said.

"It has to be drugs, ma'am. We all know drugs are coming across the border from Punjab. Why not Rajasthan?"

"Because there's a desert to cross, and the journey is much harder."

"True, but I'm thinking that perhaps they found a new route," Swati said. "What else could it be?"

"Well, the papers mention a stop on the way to Jaisalmer. There seems to be a common location just outside of Jodhpur."

"Yes, ma'am," Swati said. "I looked up the address. After a few calls to some local travel agents, I found out that it was an abandoned fort that was being used as a rest stop or fuel depot. At least, that's what I could gather from talking to transportation companies who frequent the area. The odd thing is, none of them have had any lorries there recently, but they all claimed to have seen trucks at the location. I know the info is a bit sketchy, but that's the best I could gather over the phone."

"A fort?"

"Yes, ma'am," Swati confirmed.

"Why on earth would they be stopping at an abandoned fort?" Nitya looked up to the ceiling and closed her eyes.

"Beats me." Swati shrugged. "I guess we just have to go there and find out."

Nitya turned her gaze back to Swati. Given what she would say next, she knew she had to tread carefully. "This is good, Swati. I'll read through these notes again. Is there anything else of significance?"

"Yes, ma'am," Swati responded. Turning her attention to her file, she brought out a sheet of paper from near the bottom of the pile. "Some lorries have recently left the Majestic International Hotel in Gurgaon for the same destination on the outskirts of Jaisalmer."

Nitya leaned forward, her skin prickling. That was the hotel where Kavita worked. "What about them?" Nitya asked gingerly.

"The one who signed off on them is one Nalin Kohli," Swati added.

"Hmm," mumbled Nitya. It could very well be that Nalin was in charge of signing off on shipments and deliveries at the hotel. But what Swati said next convinced her there was more to it.

"Nalin is also connected to the late Arvind Kapoor. As I mentioned, he worked at a hotel in Versova Beach before transferring to Gurgaon. He didn't leave on good terms. It seems they had some falling out," Swati said.

"How do you know?" Nitya asked.

"I managed to sneak in a short conversation with one of the receptionists in the Versova hotel. She happens to be from my batch. I didn't know her in college, but we found some common acquaintances when we started talking. When I asked about Nalin, she revealed that he was not well-liked. The rumour was that Arvind had discovered that Nalin was involved in illegal activities and was using the hotel. That didn't go down well, and he was asked to leave."

"What kind of activities?"

"She didn't say," Swati replied. "But it could have been drugs."

"That's your assumption," Nitya noted.

"Yes, ma'am. I know I shouldn't be making assumptions. But what else could it be? I mean, it's a hotel. It wouldn't be far-fetched to assume that a handful of employees are dealing drugs for their clientele," Swati reasoned. "Maybe Arvind found out, which led to the altercation that caused Nalin to flee to Delhi."

"Perhaps, but how does that tie in with Dinesh Nath? We know Nalin was acquainted with Dinesh, which was why Dinesh left Bombay. Soon afterwards, Nalin leaves Bombay and follows him here. We are still missing something," Nitya said, pacing the room.

"That's all I have, ma'am. The next step is to visit this fort in Jodhpur and see what's going on there before moving on to Jaisalmer. I'm confident the answers are there," Swati concluded, her gaze following Nitya.

Nitya stopped near the window behind her desk, her back to Swati. She peered outside on a dark, grey morning. Fog engulfed the nearby parks and buildings, and she could see silhouettes of people huddled together, enjoying warm beverages. Others hustled by in a hurry, draped in shawls, sweaters, and coats. A chill wafted over her as she turned back to Swati. She crept to the door, made sure it was firmly shut and rushed back to her chair. Once she sat down, she leaned forward and placed her hands on the table.

"Swati," Nitya whispered before raising her voice slightly. "I need to tell you something, and it must stay between us."

"Sure, ma'am," Swati mumbled. But Nitya could sense the hesitation in her voice.

"Remember when I told you I would research the partners?" Nitya continued.

Swati nodded.

"Well, that's because it bothered me that we were suddenly called back to Delhi. We were then instructed to work on another story, and I was told not to pursue this one," Nitya said.

"That bothered me, too. I wondered if our paper's owners might have something to do with Arvind Kapoor. But they don't. The Thapar brothers have no business interest in Arvind Kapoor's holdings, or those of his two partners, for that matter," Swati declared.

Nitya smiled. "I'd figured you'd look into that, but ..."

"But what, ma'am?"

"Did you know that one of Arvind's partners is related to the elder Mr Thapar's wife?"

Swati's eyes flew wide. "What?"

"Not only that, but the younger Mr Thapar's wife's family, specifically her youngest brother, is a partial factory owner that supplies parts for air coolers." Nitya paused to let her revelations sink in. Locking eyes with Swati, she continued, "Do you recall the building that held Arvind Kapoor's showroom?"

"I know a company in Bombay owns it. What are you getting at, ma'am? What did I miss?"

"Four shareholders own the company. One of them is also related to Mr Thapar's in-laws. I am not sure whether they had any knowledge of Arvind Kapoor's activities, but they certainly knew him. And ... well." Nitya sighed and paused.

"Oh! So that's the connection, you think? Are you suggesting the Thapars' extended family is involved in this conspiracy, and that was the reason they didn't want us digging any further?"

Nitya fell silent, her eyes fixed on the door. After a long minute, she mumbled, "I don't know. What else could it be?"

"But this means—" Swati blurted. Then, her eyes lowered,

flitting between her notes and the papers on the desk. Nitya knew Swati was intelligent enough to determine where this conversation was going.

"This means I can't take you to Jodhpur and Jaisalmer. You can't be part of this anymore," Nitya enunciated.

"But that's not fair! We shouldn't have to drop this just because …" Swati cried, shaking her head.

"But you know why, don't you, Swati?"

"I know, but still …"

"If things go south, and our superiors learn that not only are we disobeying their directive to prioritise another story, but that we're also working on something that might implicate the owners' families, they will come down hard on us. Only a few family-owned enterprises run the news business. If we get fired, finding a job with any of the other national papers may be tough. That's the worst-case scenario, but I have been in the news business for over a decade. Long enough to know that it is likely," Nitya stated.

"I don't know what to say," Swati whispered.

"You don't have to say anything," Nitya murmured. "I know you need this job. I also know you've done well here, and everyone—including our new bosses and owners—wants to hold on to you. Let's keep it that way."

Swati shook her head. "I pursued journalism to follow stories like this, and I enjoy working with you so much, ma'am. And now …"

"Things aren't always as they seem, Swati," Nitya said reassuringly. "I will make sure no one knows you worked with me on this. Please leave all your files and notes about Dinesh's story on my desk. Then, start working on a piece about the government contracts given to the Thapars' competitors."

"Oh, I wish it didn't have to be like this," Swati pleaded, shaking her head. "I still want to help."

"Well, there is one last thing you can do for me."

Swati jolted forward. "What is it, ma'am?"

"Find out whether any firms that won those government contracts have stakes in Rajasthan. Anything that would warrant a trip from my side to conduct further research for the story," Nitya suggested with a grin.

"Sure, ma'am. If that's the case, maybe I can join you too," blurted Swati, her eyes gleaming.

"No," Nitya said firmly. "You have been on this long enough. Besides, I don't intend to actually follow up on those contracts during my trip. It will purely be a ruse to steal away to Rajasthan, where I'll end up in Jodhpur and Jaisalmer, ostensibly to find out more about their competitors. But really, I'll be taking a closer look at those two addresses."

"Sounds a bit dicey, ma'am," Swati said.

"It is. And I fully expect everyone here to figure out my ruse eventually. They are not dumb. I'm just hoping I'll get to the truth before then," Nitya said.

"I will get you something that will justify your trip." Swati slowly got up.

"Please, close the door behind you," Nitya said, "and don't worry."

"Sure, ma'am," Swati replied. Nitya didn't miss the sad smile on her face as she left. "Good luck," she said before gently latching the door shut.

Nitya drew a deep breath and rang up Shankar.

***

Shankar marched into Gagan's office, where he found his boss with his ear glued to his phone. He sat patiently across the desk, listening to the conversation on an unrelated case. He couldn't tell whether it was a ploy by Gagan to annoy him or to give him less time to discuss the failed search in Shimla. Gagan knew what happened during his trip; Shankar was convinced of that much. But he wouldn't be caught off guard again. This time, he had a plan that would require a bit of deception and create a lot of blowback if things went wrong.

"How was Shimla?" Gagan asked, picking up a file from his desk.

"Cold, sir," Shankar said.

"It is January, and it's in the Himalayas. I'm not surprised. Did your visit help your case?"

"It did, yes," Shankar responded with practised calm.

"Oh! In what way?" Gagan's eyes widened as he placed the file he was reading back on the desk.

"I ended up talking to one of the workers, and he told me they have other locations I could check," Shankar continued.

Gagan tapped his fingers on his desk. "You found an employee in the warehouse in Shimla?"

"Not quite, sir. I stumbled upon his address in one of the many papers on the floor. I paid him a visit at his residence before returning to Delhi," Shankar lied. The response made Gagan sit upright.

"Hmm. So, where are these other warehouses?"

"In Rajasthan," Shankar replied. He watched as Gagan continued drumming his fingers on the table, then leaned forward.

"Where in Rajasthan?" Gagan demanded.

"In Pokhran and Devikot," Shankar replied, which brought a smile to Gagan's face. Shankar wondered whether his ploy had worked.

"And what do you plan to do next?"

"Go check out those locations," Shankar continued.

"Pokhran and Devikot?"

"Yes, sir," Shankar affirmed.

Gagan sighed, pausing for a moment before answering. "Sure, why not? I don't see any harm. But Shankar, you have to move on if this doesn't yield anything. We have discussed this. This case has already taken a lot of your time and far too many resources if you count on us having to send a convoy to the warehouse in Shimla. The local station called me and said that it didn't yield much. But if you say you found this employee who pointed you to the other two warehouses, I will take your word for it."

"Right, sir. You will be pleased to hear that I am prioritising another case above this one. That's why I'll be travelling to Bombay first," Shankar said solemnly.

"Oh, which one is that?"

"Narcotics, sir. If you recall, one of the places we raided during our investigation revealed that some hotels in Bombay might be hotspots for drug smuggling," Shankar added, knowing full well that Gagan rarely read files and reports in great detail.

"Well, I am pleased to hear that. Yes, this whole drug situation is another nasty business. Do you know which hotels are involved?"

"I'm hoping to get more details from the local station there," Shankar replied.

"That's good," Gagan said, his face relaxing. "Let me know if you need any help while you're there. I can talk to the commissioner if needed."

"Thank you, sir," Shankar said, secretly pleased with how things went. "There is one more thing."

"Yes?"

"I will be taking Ashok with me. I hope that's not an issue."

"Not at all. Please, do keep me posted on how things go in Bombay, Pokhran, and Devikot," Gagan said, turning his attention to the open file on his desk. Shankar nodded and left without another word.

***

When he entered his office, Shankar found Ashok pacing the length of the room.

"Sir, I have the numbers you requested," Ashok announced, placing a thick file folder on his desk. Shankar opened it and quickly sifted through the papers.

"Are they arranged by date?"

"Yes, sir," Ashok confirmed, inching closer to Shankar.

"Wonderful. Now, look at the dates just before and the day of each raid, and give me the numbers of all the outgoing calls on those days," Shankar said.

Taking the file, Ashok began picking out the pages and stacking them in a pile. "I thought we'd be confronting the person reserving the lorries or questioning the clerks to see if they or their managers were involved."

"Not so fast, Ashok. I don't want to raise any alarms just yet. We have to make sure we've got this right," Shankar warned as he carefully scanned the sheets Ashok was handing him. He circled some numbers and took his time reading and rereading the sheets. "I think I have it," Shankar said, holding the marked papers.

"I still don't get it, sir," Ashok said with a puzzled look.

"Look here. The same number was called a couple of hours before each raid. Do you see it?"

"Yes! So, whoever called this number was warning them of the upcoming raids. That's when the drivers are given the locations," Ashok said, his volume rising.

"Right. The next step is to figure out who placed the calls from our station and who was on the other side," Shankar continued.

"These calls all came from the front desk," Ashok said. "I can check the logbook to see who the duty constable was then."

"And you'll most likely see that it's the same person. I'm sure this constable made sure that he was always on duty the morning of every raid. It's easy enough to change the roster to be the duty officer. It's a thankless job, and no one ever wants to do it. We are usually informed of the raids the night before and the location the day of. As soon as he learns there will be a raid, I suspect this person does whatever it takes to put himself on duty the following morning. Once the location is shared, he calls this number"—Shankar pointed to the circles on the sheet—"to let them know the exact location."

"Wow! And that's how they always seemed to know we were coming," Ashok said.

"Yes," Shankar sighed. "They were smart to leave a bit of damning evidence and some petty miscreants in each location, just enough that the raids didn't appear to be a total loss. But that's why most supplies were gone by the time we arrived."

"And all the building owners were either never in town or claimed to be blissfully unaware of what was taking place on their premises," Ashok commented.

"Well, they are still accountable for what little we found, but their lawyers can easily argue that they were personal belongings of the individual workers and employees." Ashok picked up the papers again as Shankar spoke and paged through them.

"That still leaves the question of who they were calling."

"Right. I have a theory on that, too. We can check it out tonight," Shankar said with a smile.

Ashok raised his eyebrows. "Tonight? I can go to the telephone exchange tomorrow, as soon as possible, to ask them who this number is registered with. But it will take a while, and they will ask for a formal request, paperwork, et cetera," Ashok noted.

"Or, we could just call the number now," Shankar said. He raised his arm before Ashok could interrupt him. "Rather, *you* will call them and say that you had a package for them that you couldn't deliver because no one was at the address when you passed by this morning."

"Wouldn't that tip them off? If this number does belong to someone involved in criminal activities, it could arouse their suspicions," Ashok stated.

"True, but if my theory is correct, this number most likely doesn't belong to an individual. It is more likely a business or a public booth. Let's find out now, shall we?" Shankar said, getting up. He placed the phone on his desk and turned it toward Ashok. "I will place the call, and you do the talking. Remember, say exactly what I told you."

"Right, sir," Ashok said, his expression grave.

"Cheer up, Ashok. You are impersonating a delivery man. They are not as serious as you," Shankar said with a smile.

Ashok eased up, rolling his shoulders as Shankar dialled the number. Once he heard the click of someone picking up, he handed the receiver to Ashok. Shankar struggled not to laugh as he watched Ashok deftly negotiate his way with the person on the other end of the line. He complained about how difficult it was to find the address and how long he waited for someone to arrive. Then, he moaned about how none of the neighbours was helpful. Finally, he pretended to be angry about wasting his entire day. The whole thing went better than Shankar had anticipated, and when Ashok hung up, they both burst into laughter.

"Unbelievable," Ashok said. "So, this guy owns a sweet shop, and this number belongs to a public pay phone inside the store."

"Yes, that's what I thought," Shankar said. "I'm guessing that when the calls were placed to this number, the caller asked the booth owner to fetch someone from a nearby address. As I'm sure you know, it's common practice, and the booth owners charge a fee for the service."

"But we still don't know who the caller is asking for," Ashok said. "I suppose I could go to this sweet shop, now that I have the address, and ask the owner."

"No, that won't help," Shankar said, shaking his head. "Just look at the address—it's in Old Delhi. Each booth there gets dozens of calls every hour."

Ashok's eyes widened. "Sir, you don't think the sweet shop owner is in on this?"

"What do you think? I mean, you spoke to him," Shankar said.

"I find it unlikely, sir. At least, it didn't seem that way from how he spoke. He was fuming and couldn't fathom how I failed to find his famous shop, a landmark on his street," Ashok said with a chuckle.

"That's all right. There is another way to get to the bottom of this, but ..."

"You mean feigning a fake raid and planting someone at the store, see who they fetch once the call is placed?" Ashok asked.

"Yes. It's good to see you're thinking this through, and it may well come to that. But let's not go there just yet," Shankar said, leaning back. "We just might be able to use this to our advantage."

"How, sir?"

"You will see," Shankar said. "But now, I want you to find out—discreetly, of course—about the duty constable or constables manning the phone when these calls were placed. Learn everything you can about them."

"I'm on it," Ashok said. "Anything else, sir?"

"No, that's all for the moment," Shankar said. "I'll meet you upstairs in the records room in an hour."

Once Ashok left, Shankar pulled all the files from the folder and laid them before him. His eyes fell on a piece of paper at the corner of his desk, a note indicating that Nitya had called him twice. He called her back right away and listened patiently as her words tumbled out.

"Should I be worried?" Nitya asked once she finished, her voice shaking.

"If Nalin is still in Bombay, it should be fine. But for your sanity, have Kavita stay with a friend while you are away, preferably someone Nalin doesn't know. I can ask one of my trusted constables to check on her twice daily if that makes you feel better," Shankar said, hoping to reassure Nitya. There was a pause on the other end of the line.

"Thank you," Nitya mumbled.

"There is one thing I need to ask you, and this is for your safety. Please don't take it any other way. You know me—the last thing I want is to tell you how to do your job or impede your research in any way."

"What is it, Shankar?"

He released a deep breath. "You mentioned you're planning to visit locations in Jodhpur and Jaisalmer. My only request is that you don't go there alone. I don't need to tell you that we are dealing with something far more sinister than we had initially thought, and the folks involved have friends in high places," Shankar warned.

"I understand. I'll be careful," Nitya responded. "Anything else?"

"Yes. Please leave the name and number of the hotels you'll stay at with my assistant. I am guessing you don't have those details yet," Shankar said.

"I don't. I have to make the reservations myself, and I assume you know why," Nitya whispered.

"I know. I will be busy all day tomorrow, but I'll pick up the numbers from my secretary before I leave," Shankar said.

"Are you heading there as well?"

Shankar paused before responding. "I have to look into something else first. Depending on how things go, I might end up joining you there. When are you leaving?"

"Day after tomorrow. First, I need to ensure Kavita is safe," Nitya said.

"That's good," Shankar replied. "Well, I need to get going. If there's anything, please call me at my home number tonight."

"Thank you, Shankar."

"Stay safe, and out of trouble." With those words of caution, he hung up. His next call was to the Rajasthan Police, and after a long conversation, he called the Andheri Police Station in Bombay.

Another hour passed before he got up to search for Ashok. Shankar found him smoking a cigarette beneath a tree near the gate. He marched up to him, and together, they headed to the records room on the station's top floor.

"Deepak Kumar, sir," Ashok said in a hushed tone.

"What's that?"

"The name of the duty constable when the calls were placed," Ashok muttered, darting glances in all directions.

"No one else at that time?"

"No, sir," Ashok confirmed. "I know him personally—he's from my village. But I'd have never guessed he was the snitch. However, I should have suspected something. He was showing off an expensive watch and a new scooter. He told me they were gifts from relatives, and I didn't think much of it."

"Well, that's the way it goes sometimes. Anyhow, there's something else we need to focus on," Shankar said before carefully laying out his plan.

"The whole day at the library, sir?" Ashok's shoulders drooped as he stood across from Shankar, who was poring over files on a dimly lit table. He hunched over to scrutinise the handwritten notes and typewritten pages. The solitary lamp on the desk was hardly enough to illuminate their distant corner.

"Yes, Ashok, the entire day. Is this everything on Arvind Kapoor and his partners that you could dig up in the archives?" Shankar asked, pointing to the box from which he had picked the files.

"Yes, sir."

Shankar released a puff of air. "All right. I'll have to go through these tonight. What about your search for Aria among the adoption agencies? Any record of her?"

"No, sir. But it is possible she was adopted from an agency elsewhere. Dinesh and his wife did meet in Bombay. They may have used an agency there, and before you ask, I am also checking those," Ashok responded.

"Good work," Shankar said. "Now, I need you to pack your bags. We are heading to Bombay tomorrow night after our library stint."

Ashok guffawed, his eyes wide. "Bombay?"

"I will fill you in on the way," Shankar said, putting the file back in the box. He switched off the table lamp, picked up the box, and retreated to his office with Ashok close behind. Once there, he called Bharat at the library to tell him they would visit the following day and that they should be undisturbed during their stay. Then, he asked Bharat to compile a list of all the books Dinesh had borrowed over the last few months and have it ready when they arrived.

***

Shankar and Ashok were among the first visitors to the library. They planted themselves across a large desk in one corner facing the hall. They had a clear view of the main entrance and the entire ground floor from this vantage point.

"What exactly are we looking for, sir?"

"Any activity that seems out of the norm for a library," Shankar responded, glancing around. A few old men sat around a desk near the newspaper and magazine aisle. The staff were busy stacking returned books in their designated spots. Meanwhile, Bharat was marshalling the two clerks at the counter to keep the catalogue in order.

"We can't see the upper floor from here, sir," Ashok commented.

"I am aware of that," Shankar said. "But we can see if anyone's heading that way," he continued, pointing to the two winding metal staircases that spiralled to the upper section and the elevator behind the counter. "If anyone goes there, one of us will follow."

"Understood, sir." Ashok nodded.

"Now, go find yourself some books and magazines so people think you're reading," Shankar whispered with a smile. Then, he reached into his bag and brought a heavy file and a stack of papers.

"Right, sir," sighed Ashok. "I never even spent this much time in the library as a student. Now, I have to spend an entire day here," he muttered.

Shankar smirked. "And you will *still* not be studying."

Ashok shook his head, breathed a long sigh, and stalked away. Shankar draped his jacket over the back of his chair before getting up and heading to the counter. He picked up the list Bharat had compiled and surveyed the hall from this new vantage point. A few students were trickling in and easing themselves into cushioned chairs beside his and Ashok's table. Seeing students without their uniforms on a school day wasn't surprising. Many were busy studying for the countrywide board examinations, and most schools gave them a few weeks off to prepare.

Satisfied, Shankar turned to a section behind a table where a gentleman who looked like a professor was sitting. A young man ran his finger along a row of book spines, probably looking for a specific title—nothing unusual.

Shankar ambled back to the large table in the corner, where he found Ashok sitting with a stack of magazines, newspapers, and comics before him.

"Really, Ashok. You couldn't find a book?" whispered Shankar as he sat opposite his constable. Ashok was sifting through his pile, trying to find something to read. Shankar sighed. "You'll be better off sitting over there," Shankar added, pointing to the side of the table that offered a clearer view.

"Right, sir." He quickly picked up his pile and moved. Once he settled in, he continued, "If Gagan Ji and others in our station knew I was spending my day reading comics and magazines at the library, I wouldn't hear the end of it."

Shankar laughed. "Just blame it on me. And trust me, if they do find out, I promise not to mention that you've been reading Bollywood gossip and Amar Chitra Katha."

Sharing a chuckle, they both started reading, stealing glances at every newcomer. The morning passed by in relative quiet, with only a few people coming to read the newspapers and then leaving. The students whispered among themselves while studying, and Bharat had to warn them a few times to maintain silence. All the while, Shankar kept a watchful eye in all directions. After three hours, he noticed Ashok tapping his feet under the table.

"What's wrong?"

"Nothing, sir. I am just not used to being on duty without my uniform. You look strange, too. I mean, this is not normal for us, sitting in a library, watching old people reading and students studying. I haven't seen anything unusual."

"Let's stay focused, shall we?" Shankar whispered.

"On what exactly, sir?"

"The section right behind those two gentlemen over there," Shankar replied, jerking his chin toward a table a few feet away.

"There's no one there," Ashok declared.

"Right, but since we've arrived, a few people have stopped by at regular intervals—half an hour apart. They've drawn out a book, placed something in it, and left. Then, the next person comes and does the same thing."

Ashok's eyebrows drew together in puzzlement. "Okay. I will stay focused on that section."

"Good. Now, let me confirm something in the catalogue. Then, I'll make a quick trip to the upper floor and return shortly," Shankar said. "Remember, just observe from afar. Is that understood?"

"Yes, sir," Ashok said with a curt nod.

Shankar shuffled over to the tall drawers holding the library catalogue. Carefully checking the list Bharat had compiled, he scribbled their locations on the paper. He then craned his neck to glimpse Ashok, still chipping away at his pile of magazines, darting glances toward the section Shankar had pointed out.

Climbing the winding staircase to the upper floor, Shankar checked a few books in each aisle and then scrutinised the area as a whole. This was a smaller section, with fewer desks and no one studying or reading.

Satisfied, he headed back down and walked up to the main counter. Bharat sat behind his sprawling mahogany desk, poring over a large sheet. Shankar tapped on the counter. When Bharat looked up, Shankar pointed to the small administration room behind a water cooler. They moseyed over there, and once they were inside, Shankar quickly lowered the blinds and shut the door.

"Bharat Ji, I want you to think very carefully before answering the questions I am about to pose," Shankar started.

"Of course, sir," Bharat mumbled.

"You told us that Dinesh failed to show up to work one day, and you also didn't see him at his apartment," Shankar continued.

"That's right, sir."

"So, when was the last time you saw Dinesh? Was it at his apartment or here at work?"

"Here at the library, sir," Bharat responded quickly. "He came to work on Saturday just before we closed, and I never saw him again."

"I am sorry to be harping on this, Bharat Ji, but are you sure that you didn't see him back at his apartment or noticed anything that would indicate that he ever returned, like his lights being on?" Shankar inquired.

"Correct, sir," Bharat responded. "If you recall, the table lamp in his apartment was still on, but that isn't unusual."

Shankar began pacing the length of the little room. He stroked his chin, peered at the door, and then turned to the old librarian.

"When you arrived here on Sunday morning, the day after Dinesh went missing, was anything different? Odd?"

Bharat paused, closing his eyes as if deep in thought. He opened his eyes, looked to the corner of the room, and then snapped his fingers. "Yes! And I mentioned this to Hritesh as well."

"What was it?"

"The lights, and his flashlight and lunchbox," Bharat blurted, his words jumbled.

"I am sorry, I don't understand."

"When we came in on Sunday morning, we found the lights on in the main hall, that one over there," Bharat said, pointing to a large chandelier hanging from the middle of the ceiling. "Dinesh never leaves them on, ever. We also found his flashlight on the counter. He always kept it with him and took it home at night's end. He also left his lunchbox here. Usually, he brought some snacks with him."

"Was it empty?" Shankar asked.

Bharat squinted, his brow wrinkled. "Sorry?"

"Was the lunchbox empty? Did he eat anything?"

"Oh, yes. We only found a banana peel and a peanut bag. Nothing else inside, just the wrapper," Bharat said. "If you want to take a look, I can show it to you."

"Yes, in a minute," Shankar said. Drawing a deep breath, he prepared to ask his next question. The one to which he already knew the answer but wanted Bharat to confirm. "Do you have any cameras inside or outside the building?"

"We are not a bank or a museum, sir. We don't have a single camera. And honestly, we haven't had any theft-related issues for as long as I can remember."

"All right. One last question, and then we will check out Dinesh's lunchbox." Shankar touched his thumb to his chin.

"I am sure you get a few regulars in the library. Are there any individuals who come here often but don't borrow books? Or have never borrowed books, ever?"

Bharat smiled. "Of course. This is a public library. Several people come here regularly, and many just come to read and then leave. Nothing peculiar about that, is there?"

"I suppose you're right," Shankar said, agreeing. Bharat's response was precisely what he was expecting. Unfortunately, it wasn't exactly helpful.

He swung the door open and followed Bharat to an open locker. There, the librarian pulled out a lunchbox and a flashlight and placed them on a small desk. Shankar examined them carefully and then glanced up at Bharat.

"If you don't mind, I'd like to keep these to see if they aid the investigation." Once Bharat nodded his consent, Shankar hustled back to where Ashok was supposed to be seated. Instead, Ashok stood at the section he was instructed to observe, his eyes searching.

"Sir," Ashok started loudly, which made the patrons at the nearest table turn to glare at them. "Sorry," Ashok babbled before guiding Shankar to a corner well out of earshot.

"You weren't supposed to leave the desk. What are you doing here?" Shankar hissed.

"I am sorry, sir. I think I made a mistake. A gentleman came by and tucked what looked like a note and a photograph inside a book, then left. A few minutes later, another gentleman came and seemed to take out the same book. He read the note and ..."

"And what?" Shankar demanded.

"Before leaving, he glanced around and saw me staring at him. Then, he panicked and left with the contents, I think," Ashok added sheepishly.

"Ashok!" Shankar groaned, shaking his head. "Now they

know we're on to them. They won't come back here anymore."

"I am sorry, sir," Ashok said with a trembling voice, his eyes trained on the floor.

Shankar sighed. "All right, we can't go back and change what happened. Let's talk about what you saw. Can you identify the two men?"

"Yes, sir," Ashok replied hurriedly.

"Good. Now, about this note and photo. Was the book in that section?" Shankar asked, pointing to the area they had just come from.

"Yes, sir and I can even tell you which book," Ashok confidently added.

"Here's what we'll do—check all the books in that section and see if anything is inserted. If we find any loose notes, scraps, or photos, we take them with us," Shankar stated.

"Good plan, sir," Ashok said. Marching back to the aisle, they carefully pulled out and paged through all the books in the section. After almost an hour, Ashok found nothing but a piece of paper with some digits scribbled.

Shankar had no such luck. From the worn spines and crumpled pages of a few books, he could see that items had been placed and removed frequently. Giving up on the fruitless search, he told Ashok to head outside. It was late afternoon, and the skies were overcast. Shankar surveyed the gardens and sat down at a small picnic table.

"I think we're done with our work inside ..." Shankar started.

"I am sorry, sir. My excitement got the better of me. I know I probably botched our stakeout," Ashok uttered, his gaze falling to the table.

"That's all right, Ashok," Shankar said. Leaning forward, he detailed everything he had learned from Bharat.

When he finished, Ashok sat back, crossing his arms over his chest. "What does this all mean?"

"We will get to that in a minute. I have here the list of books that Dinesh borrowed," Shankar said, handing it to Ashok.

His eyes roved back and forth. "They don't have anything in common. Books on astronomy, music, religion, sports—he is all over the place."

"True, they have nothing in common except where they are in the library," Shankar said.

"The same section we were watching!" Ashok said, snapping his fingers.

"Yes," Shankar confirmed.

"That's why you went to check the catalogue, sir."

"Correct. Now, that piece of paper you found. Do you know what it signifies?" Shankar continued.

"No, sir. It looks like a bunch of digits, two numbers with a comma in between. Initially, I thought it could be a sum, an amount of money, for example. But the format is all off. It also doesn't look like a phone number," Ashok mused, shaking his head slowly.

"They're latitudes and longitudes for a specific location. I bet this one points to another warehouse or an address in Rajasthan or Bombay. We will take a look once we get back to the office," Shankar said.

Ashok breathed a long exhale. "Exchanging notes, photos, location coordinates—this is quite an elaborate operation for drug dealing."

"We're not certain it's drugs," Shankar said, bringing his eyes to the gate. He gestured to the exit, and they got up to loiter outside the main entrance with the facade of the building behind them.

"Perhaps it's artefacts. In Rajasthan, some gangs deal in

antiquities and sell them across the border," Ashok declared. "Or, it could be arms or weapons. Think about it. Over the years, the Border Security Force has nabbed quite a few miscreants trying to smuggle arms across the border."

"That is possible. Then again ..." Shankar stopped, deciding it was finally time to let Ashok in on his theory. "I believe the gang is using this library not for your day-to-day dealing but for a more complex clandestine sales operation."

"How so, sir?"

"The buyers and sellers use notes and photos to exchange information on the merchandise, price, and location of the goods. Libraries are public places, easy to mingle in, and quiet. I believe the buyers and sellers never meet face-to-face, which explains why they showed up at different times. Only a select few know about the entire operation. That's what I wanted to sniff out," Shankar stated.

Ashok's face fell. "I understand, sir. I apologise. . ."

"Don't. Not all is lost. We know what they are doing now, and that's a good start. We will get them, don't worry," Shankar said, casting him a reassuring smile. A silence hung over them for a minute.

"Are we done here, sir?" Ashok asked, motioning to the library.

"Not quite," Shankar mumbled. The wind had picked up, gusts swirling around them. Suddenly, the skies looked ominous. Ashok shivered as he held on tightly to his coat.

"What is it, sir?"

"We have looked for Dinesh everywhere except here," Shankar said, gesturing to the grounds around the library.

"What? You mean, here in the library? But ..." His eyes widened. "Oh!"

"Yes," Shankar whispered. "I am beginning to think he might be dead, though I hope I am wrong."

Ashok stared back, his face ashen.

"Here's what I suspect. Dinesh found out about this entire operation and was about to tell the police, or maybe he discussed it with his wife, a constable in the Rajasthan Police. That was his undoing," Shankar said in a solemn voice.

Ashok shook his head. "You think his wife and daughter ..."

"I can't be sure. But we need to search the grounds." Shankar turned sideways and took a few steps, pointing to the landscaped area lining the building. "Let's start with the garden and the paths on this side, and we'll mirror our search afterwards. If we don't find anything, we'll expand past the property beyond the gate."

"Right, sir." Ashok nodded and stepped toward the path. They spent the next hour peering behind every hedge, bush, and tree, scouring the area for any marks or freshly disturbed soil, but they found nothing. Even as it started raining, Shankar insisted that they continue.

After a few more minutes, they reached the end of the property behind the building—a path lined with overgrown weeds led to an abandoned shed beneath an old tree. Shankar and Ashok glanced at one another, then crept along the waterlogged path. Once they reached the shed, they skirted around it. It was utterly boarded up on all sides, and they struggled to find an opening through the curtain of trees and vines that crept up the walls.

"There." Shankar pointed to a horizontal plank that appeared loose. "That board looks like it was recently nailed in," he said as he grabbed the side of the plank and pulled.

After a few firm tugs, the plank started wobbling. Ashok took over, prying it off the exterior. They peeked inside, and the first thing that hit Shankar was the smell. It was nauseating. Shankar and Ashok kicked at another plank. Coming loose, it created an opening large enough for them to crawl through.

Shankar went in first, with Ashok following close behind. Once inside, the stench was overbearing. They pulled out their handkerchiefs and bundled them over their mouths and noses. Shankar couldn't see anything in the dark interior. The vegetation enveloping the structure prevented any light from filtering through.

"Do you have a flashlight?" Shankar asked.

Ashok brought out a small torch, shining it toward the smell. He let out a gasp, and the flashlight fell from his hand. He stumbled back through the opening and ran outside. The sound of his retching struck Shankar's ears. Carefully, he picked up the flashlight from the ground and shone it toward the other end of the room.

A rotting corpse in a security guard's uniform stared back at him, a large gash marring its forehead and chest. Shankar moved closer, only to find Dinesh Nath's name tag attached to the dead man's tunic.

Cargo

Nitya checked into the guesthouse in Jodhpur around midnight, exhausted from her long journey. Perched amid the stark landscape of the Thar Desert, the aptly named "Blue City" looked magnificent even at night. Nitya chose a small boutique hotel in the old city across from the ancient Mehrangarh Fort. The famous landmark was surrounded by steep walls and gates. As for the hotel itself, it was popular among tourists, and Nitya had selected it by design so she could join one of the many daily excursions led by local guides.

She called to check on Kavita as soon as she arrived and settled in for the night. Her room was tastefully decorated, its walls painted a deep blue with drapes and bed sheets in the same shade. A small, ornate desk with a table lamp and a vase filled with orchids topped off the elegant look. Sprawling on her large bed, Nitya tucked her head against one of the pillows and opened the small map that Swati had given her. The next thing she remembered was waking up to the morning sunlight streaming through the open windows, reflecting on the large mirror opposite her bed.

Before heading down for breakfast, Nitya talked to the concierge about joining a guided tour of all the forts and palaces in the city—including the one marked on the map. The concierge divulged that it was an abandoned palace, not frequented by travellers or locals, and that it wasn't a sought-after attraction in the city. Not deterred, Nitya insisted that they visit the landmark.

To sweeten the pot, she showed him her credentials as a journalist and revealed that she was doing a piece on boutique hotels and historical forts in Jodhpur. The man's face lit up immediately. He scrambled to get on the phone with the guide, ordering her to cater to Nitya's requests during the tour.

Happy with the outcome, she hopped to the restaurant and dove into a sumptuous breakfast of bajra roti, chutney, kami vada, and egg bhurji. She couldn't recall the last time she'd taken a vacation alone. Though this wasn't a holiday, her surroundings made her feel like she was in the midst of one. Growing up, her parents and sisters were her regular travel companions, and more recently, either Kavita or Jai would accompany her during weekend getaways outside Delhi.

Donning her sunglasses, she quickly found her tour guide and group. Her fellow travellers were a mix of Indians and foreigners, all couples except one large family. A middle-aged man with a bored expression, travelling with his wife, started a conversation with Nitya. Within minutes, she knew everything there was to know about him. The guide led them into a small, air-conditioned minivan, and they took off for their first stop—Mandore Fort.

The historic site was situated five miles outside the city in an ancient village. Their over-enthusiastic guide, armed with a microphone, enchanted her audience with the city's history and stories about its landmarks. She was careful to address every question, especially Nitya's frequent inquiries. By lunchtime, they had already covered Mandore, Kherjala, and Chanwa forts. They then stopped at a restaurant popular with tourists and tour operators. While the rest of the group split off to dine as couples, Nitya headed to the table where their guide, Pari, was seated.

"Mind if I join you?" Nitya asked.

"Not all, Nitya Ji," Pari said, getting up.

"No, no need for that. Stay seated, please," Nitya said, sitting across from her. The restaurant was brimming with travellers. Luckily, Nitya didn't have to place an order since the tour package had a set menu. While they waited for the food to arrive, Nitya noticed Pari fiddling with her pen, darting glances toward the rest of their group. "Everything all right?" Nitya asked.

"Yes, ma'am. I'm just making sure I know where everyone is and that the food arrives on time," Pari said quickly, smiling. Soon, the waiter arrived with their vegetarian thalis. Pari craned her neck to make sure everyone else had gotten their food. Seemingly satisfied, she finally settled down.

"Don't worry, Pari. Everything will be fine," Nitya said, picking up a puri and dipping it into her aloo gobi.

"Thank you, ma'am. It's just that we have an evening tour after this, and I have to be back in time to make sure the driver and the minivan are ready," she said before digging into her food.

"Does that tour make the same stops?"

"No, ma'am. That one stops at all the temples in the city. They are illuminated at night. The forts are, too, but only from the outside, and not all of them. They are pretty to look at from afar, but you can't see much in the dark when you go inside," Pari said before taking another bite.

"How long have you been doing this? Guiding tours, I mean."

"Since I graduated, ma'am, so almost two years now," Pari responded.

"You have quite a knack for it. I can see that," Nitya said, arching her eyebrows as she sipped water. Before she could continue, Pari spoke up.

"Thank you. It's not what I want to do, but there aren't many options for arts graduates. I am preparing for the civil services exam. This is mainly just to earn some income and keep me afloat for now," the young guide explained.

"Are you from Jodhpur originally?"

"I am, and I live with my parents. But they are teachers, and their salaries don't ... well, you know how it goes," Pari added.

"Well, I am glad you are ambitious and trying to get ahead. From what I can tell, you are smart and resourceful. I am confident you will do well," Nitya said with a genuine smile.

"Thank you, ma'am. At the hotel, they told me you are a journalist. Which paper, if I may ask?"

"*The Daily Citizen News*," Nitya responded.

Pari's eyes sparkled. "Oh, I know that one. It's one of the largest dailies in the country. Wow! You must be good. I haven't come across many female reporters," Pari bubbled.

"There weren't many when I started in a small regional newspaper more than a decade ago. But things are changing. More women are joining the ranks. But progress is much slower than it should be if you ask me," Nitya remarked.

"How did you manage it, maintaining a career for so long? It must be a lot of work, and then there must be juggling expectations from the family. It can't be easy," Pari continued.

"Oh, I am not married," Nitya responded. "And yes, it is a lot of work, with long hours, but it's rewarding. There are good days and bad. Most importantly, I love it, and there's nothing else I'd rather be doing."

Pari's eyes grew wide. "Wow. I don't think I could ever get my parents to see things that way. They are already on my case about getting married. Just getting them to agree to hold off until I am more independent was a huge thing," Pari muttered.

"I can imagine. Trust me, I'm the eldest of three sisters, and I am the biggest disappointment because I am not married. My youngest sister is divorced, and the other is a happily married housewife. My mother takes every opportunity to dish out unsolicited advice and snide remarks on how I should be more like her," Nitya said.

"That must be hard." Her face brightened. "From now on, I will keep an eye out for the pieces you write, Nitya Ji," she said. Glancing at Nitya's map on the table, she pointed to the marked spot. "Why that fort?"

Nitya shrugged. "Why not?"

Pari pursed her lips. "There are six forts in Jodhpur, the three we saw this morning and three more we will visit after lunch. There are, of course, other smaller mahals, but they are mostly just stones and dirt in the middle of barren sand and overgrown vegetation. Your requested stop lies on the way to the Umaid Bhawan Palace. I have gone past the fort a few times, and on several occasions, I stopped briefly for folks to take pictures, but there isn't much to see."

"Well, it was recommended by one of my friends who is into photography. I just want to snap some pictures. It shouldn't take long."

"Sure, ma'am," Pari said, her tone brimming with enthusiasm. They spent the next few minutes polishing off their thalis. When the waiter came by again, he served them some creamy lassi and plates of syrupy gulab jamuns, which they eagerly devoured after the spicy lunch fare. Pari and Nitya glanced at the rest of their group, who were also enjoying their sweets.

"What's this fort called?" Nitya asked, pointing to the location on the map she had once again unfolded after the waiter cleaned the table.

"It's neither a fort nor a palace, and if you see it now, it's nothing but a sad, roofless structure forgotten amid a sandy stretch of land. It's called Kangra Mahal and was built as a guesthouse for royals visiting Jodhpur from Kangra. The royal families of Jodhpur and Kangra were connected via marriage. At some point, one of Umaid Singh's ministers erected a dedicated guesthouse for visitors from Kangra. Hence, the name," Pari explained.

Before Nitya could ask her next question, the driver came by to tell Pari that they should get moving. Hopping up from the table, she immediately marshalled the rest of the group into the minivan, and they drove to their next stop—Rohet Garh Fort, a spectacular structure built in the early seventeenth century. Nitya took some photos as "oohs" and "aahs" rose from the rest of her group.

Their next destination was Kangra Mahal. After witnessing Rohet Garh, the contrast was stark. It looked even more run-down and dilapidated than Nitya had imagined. Pari asked the driver to stop in front of the old stone building, and Nitya could tell by the tourists' confused faces that they were wondering why they were stopping. The wind had picked up, and the sand around the rugged mahal began swirling into dust devils and blowing in their direction.

Stepping out and shielding her face, Nitya hustled up to two gentlemen still seated, camera straps draped over their necks. In a hushed voice, she suggested there were nice shots to be taken. They exited the van and followed Pari and Nitya toward the main entrance, a stone arch with no doors. The facade, with its rough stones, exuded an imposing aura even though it was falling apart.

As they neared the building, Nitya was surprised to find people filing in and out of a makeshift gate that looked like a new addition. *Why construct a gate around a structure that is falling to pieces?* Nitya wondered. She tried to peer beyond the gates. The structure's walls were crumbling, with much of the roof absent. Only one of the four rounded turrets was intact. Inside the tower, two people looked into the large, unkempt yard where Nitya and the rest stood. A handful of other people were stationed at the open archway. They didn't look like tourists.

"That's a bit strange. I wouldn't have expected to find anyone here," Pari said.

"Who are these people?" Nitya asked.

"As far as I know, the place isn't occupied. And I have been inside—there are no amenities," Pari continued. "I wonder who they are."

Nitya and the two gentlemen accompanying them started snapping pictures. That had an immediate effect on the people watching them from the gate, who marched up to Nitya's group and started yelling in Hindi for them to put down their cameras and be on their way. Their menacing tone cut through the air, and they carried heavy lathis, wielding the long wooden batons with practised ease. Pari held up her hands, smiling disarmingly.

"Gentlemen, we're only passing by to see the fort as part of our tour."

That didn't seem to pacify them. One of them stomped up to Pari. "This area is off limits due to an event," he blurted while the other shouted, "It's a movie shoot for a Bollywood film."

Nitya pestered them with questions, but the men did not respond. The altercation had drawn the attention of Nitya's group, who had now gathered around them. Over the din of the argument, a loud voice rang out from Kangra Mahal. A tall gentleman strode out and ordered the two men to turn back.

The gentleman ambled up to Pari, and the two started talking. Nitya seized her chance to peek into the wide entrance and then toward the broken wall on the side of the building. Through the gaping hole, she noticed that a few tents had been erected inside. Some small lorries were parked toward one side, and men carried large containers normally used for catering weddings in and out of the tents.

She pulled her eyes away when Pari addressed the rest of the group, requesting that they leave for their next destination. The entire experience left a bad taste in their mouths, and in the minivan, Nitya overheard a hushed conversation regarding the strange and unpleasant encounter. Sitting next to Pari, Nitya saw the young travel guide trembling, darting glances toward the group and shaking her head.

"It's all right, Pari," Nitya soothed.

"I don't know, ma'am. I've never had such an experience before," Pari said, bouncing her knees and tapping her fingers on her lap.

"What did that man tell you?"

"He threatened to call my tour company and complain that the driver and I brought all of you here," Pari said. "He was surprised that this place was one of the stops on the tour."

"Did he identify himself?"

"No. He just told me that the building was off limits because of an event, basically warning me that we should leave if we didn't want further trouble," Pari added.

"Really? What kind of event?"

"I don't know, maybe a movie shoot or a wedding? I was too scared to ask," Pari whimpered.

Nitya drew a sigh. "I am sorry I put you in that situation."

"It's not your fault. I mean, I have been there before. This has never happened, ever."

"Well, I can tell you there were no cameras or posters. It was neither a movie shoot nor a wedding. There's something else going on," Nitya concluded.

Pari leaned closer, her eyes wide. "What?"

"I don't know. But don't you worry about it. Just pull yourself together and finish the tour," Nitya said, placing a hand on Pari's shoulder. The young tour guide smiled and nodded.

Luckily, the beauty and breathtaking grandeur of Umaid Palace and Mehrangarh Fort made everyone forget their sour experience at Kangra Mahal. After soaking in the panoramic desert view from the fifteenth-century Mehrangarh Fort, the tourists relegated that unpleasant moment to memory. When the tour ended, they showered Pari with compliments and praise.

Once they returned to the guesthouse, Nitya approached the two tourists who had taken pictures with her at Kangra Mahal. She asked if she might take their camera rolls for development, only to compare photos, and offered to pay for a rapid film-processing service at a photo store across from the guesthouse. They agreed, and within a few hours, Nitya had all the copies she needed to uncover what was going on inside the mahal that they had been chased away from.

She lay all the photos on the bed and scrutinised them individually. Taking out a magnifying glass, an accessory she always carried that had come in handy on many occasions, she pored over each picture. Her gaze fell on two shots that had captured the interior of one of the tents through a narrow opening.

Although the photograph was grainy, and the inside of the tent was dark compared to the rest of the picture, the sunlight seeping through the crack was enough to reveal what it held. She studied the picture and then examined the first one again. As she did, she played out everything that had happened in Delhi, Gurgaon, and Shimla. She swallowed hard, her throat like sandpaper. They had it all wrong. She finally knew what the gang was smuggling, and the answer made her heart quicken.

***

Arriving in Bombay, Shankar and Ashok began their drive to the Andheri Police Station. One of Shankar's fellow officers had been entrusted with the investigation into Dinesh's death, freeing him up to continue his pursuit. While stuck in traffic, Shankar noticed Ashok lifting his bulky camera to snap a few pictures.

"First time in Bombay?" Shankar asked.

"Yes, sir," Ashok said, putting his camera down when the Jeep started moving again.

"What are your first impressions?"

"Grand city, more crowded than New Delhi, but the smell, sir," Ashok said.

"Yes, the smell of the sea." Shankar smiled.

"And salt, and fish, and ... I don't know. Don't people in the city smell it?"

Shankar laughed, and from the corner of his eye, he also saw the driver smiling. "I am sure they do, Ashok, but they've gotten used to it. I am sure folks in Bombay would say the same about the smog in Delhi during the winter."

"True, sir."

When they reached the station, Shankar was struck by the stark contrast between this building and his station in New Delhi. The freshly painted building stood in a busy commercial area surrounded by shops, offices, and high-rises. They were ushered into a spacious office. The nameplate on the door read "Anjali Gupta." Ashok reread it a few times before entering, which brought a smile to Shankar's face.

"A lady police officer, sir," Ashok remarked as they sat down side by side in front of a large, clean desk, which held two phones on one side and a notepad on the other. Large portraits of Gandhi and Nehru stared down at them from behind Anjali's cushioned chair. The lone window in the room was wide open, and sunlight poured in.

Shankar grinned. "Yes, Ashok. She is a senior officer, the same rank as me, but two years more senior. You'd better get used to it. It's a whole new world."

"Where are her files? I mean, look at her desk," Ashok whispered, pointing to her chair and the pristine glass desktop.

"A messy desk isn't necessarily a sign of a large workload, or, for that matter, a reflection on an officer's efficiency," Shankar said.

"But—" Ashok stopped at the sound of the door opening. He immediately got up, and they both turned around to see Anjali walking toward them in a bright yellow sari. After greeting them warmly, she ordered some tea, and once they all settled into their chairs, she was the first to broach the subject at hand.

"I gather you are here to know how things are progressing on the drug-smuggling case?"

"Yes, ma'am," Shankar said.

"Call me Anjali," she said with a smile. "And I hope you don't mind if I call you by your first name."

"Not at all," Shankar replied. He turned to Ashok, who looked on with wide eyes and nodded.

Shankar wondered how much she knew about what happened in Delhi. Gagan would have already spoken to her superiors about Shankar's visit, and they would have probably filled her in.

"Well, I have the list of hotels you requested. I am surprised that your superiors would send you from Delhi to pursue one of our cases," Anjali remarked, leaning back in her chair.

"We are not here to encroach on your jurisdiction, and we certainly don't want to jeopardise your investigation," Shankar said.

Anjali nodded. Reaching into a drawer on the side of her desk, she brought out a file. She paged through it, took out a sheet of paper, and handed it to Shankar. Their tea arrived, and while the attendant was pouring it, Shankar read the list carefully before giving it to Ashok.

"As you can imagine, many of these properties are under active surveillance, and we also have some informants. If you go around questioning the hotel personnel, they may become wary," Anjali continued.

"I understand. Please, let me assure you that we will not do anything to set off any alarms."

"I appreciate that," Anjali said. She gestured to Shankar's tea, and they paused to take a few sips. Meanwhile, Ashok finished reading the list and handed it back to Anjali.

"Oh, that's for you." Anjali held up a palm to stop him.

"Thank you, Anjali Ji," Ashok said, tucking the list in his bag and reaching for his teacup.

"Is there anything else I can help you with?" Anjali intertwined her fingers over her desk.

"Yes," Shankar replied, taking on a more serious tone. "One of the cases that landed in our station regards the disappearance of one Mr Dinesh Nath. He worked as a night watchman in a library and as a guard at a Delhi warehouse. Before that, he lived here in Bombay. He worked at the showroom owned by Arvind Kapoor, who I believe was murdered a few days ago."

"Yes, I am aware of that case, and as you know, we are still looking into Arvind's death. One of my colleagues is leading the investigation. You think there is a connection between the narcotics case and what happened to Mr Kapoor?"

"I don't know for sure, but it's possible," Shankar continued.

Anjali tilted her head to the side. "What makes you say that?"

"As you may be aware, the warehouse we inspected before we visited Bombay belongs to Arvind and his partners," Shankar started.

"The same warehouse that Mr Nath worked in?" Anjali leaned forward.

"Yes, although I can't be sure, I think Dinesh may have uncovered something illegal at the warehouse. He could have been planning to go to the police but didn't get the chance."

"Illegal, as in storing and transporting drugs?"

"Maybe. Or something else," Shankar said.

"Hmm," Anjali mumbled, furrowing her brow as she became lost in thought.

"There is another thing," Shankar added, pointing to Ashok's bag where he'd placed the list from Anjali.

"What's that?"

"The list you shared with us doesn't include the hotel in Versova Beach, the one owned by Arvind Kapoor and his partners," Shankar said.

"I know. That's because we haven't had any reason to believe it's a hotspot for drug dealing," Anjali concluded. She narrowed her eyes. "But you are suggesting something else altogether, aren't you? This isn't about drugs at all. What am I missing?"

"I am sure you read about the raids and the drugs we hauled in. It was all in the papers," Shankar said.

Anjali nodded. "Yes, I am aware. Your superiors shared the details with us."

"Didn't it strike you as odd that, given the wide net we had cast, we only managed to apprehend a meagre drug cache, and the folks we nabbed were all low-level operatives and dealers?" Shankar added.

Anjali locked eyes with Shankar. "Are you suggesting what I think you are suggesting, Shankar? Because if you are, and you are wrong, you are treading on thin ice."

Shankar shrugged and wore a smile. "I am not suggesting

anything. I'm just saying that it's worth looking into."

"There must be something else that led you to believe this. It couldn't have just been Dinesh Nath," Anjali remarked.

"A source told me that Arvind had a falling out with another employee who worked in his hotel in Versova Beach. This employee, Nalin Kohli, threatened Dinesh Nath and his family while they were in Bombay. Dinesh then took his family to Delhi, and Nalin followed him there." Shankar turned to Ashok, who handed him a file. Shankar pulled out a sheet and passed it to Anjali. "These are the details of Nalin Kohli. He works at a hotel in Delhi. It's all in the file. What we know is that he is now in Bombay."

"What's the connection to Arvind Kapoor, apart from him being a disgruntled employee?" asked Anjali, reading over Nalin's details.

"As it turns out, he's a distant relative of Arvind Kapoor," Shankar said.

"Oh! I certainly wasn't aware of that. We will look into this Nalin and his connection to Mr Kapoor as part of our investigation," Anjali said. "And you think Nalin may be connected to Arvind's death?"

"To be clear, Nalin himself was in Delhi when Arvind Kapoor was killed. And we haven't found anything that would suggest he was responsible for Dinesh's death either. All we know is that he threatened Dinesh and his family, and he hurried back to Bombay once he heard that Arvind had died," Shankar noted.

"Understood, and I am sure your station is investigating Dinesh's murder now."

"We are," Shankar confirmed.

Anjali stared down at her desk. "So, Arvind Kapoor not only fell out with his partners but also with Nalin Kohli." As she spoke, Shankar shared a glance with Ashok.

"I assume you are already investigating that as a possible motive?" Shankar asked, quickly adding, "The fact that he may have fallen out with his partners."

Anjali nodded. "It's been a frustrating case. So far, we haven't found anything conclusive. The statements we have taken are all hearsay and opinion. The partners have lawyered up, and what little we have uncovered until now would never hold up in court. However, this link to Nalin and Dinesh gives us a new lead. We will see where it gets us."

"Thank you, Anjali," Shankar said before finishing his tea.

Anjali got up and strode over to the open window. She gazed out with her back toward Shankar and Ashok, her vibrant sari gleaming in the sunlight. Then, she turned to Shankar and smirked. "I think I know why you came to Bombay."

Shankar kept quiet, and Ashok shifted his weight from one leg to another. When Anjali looked at Ashok, Shankar turned to him as well. "Ashok, can you give us a minute, please?"

"Yes, sir," Ashok responded, getting up. Before leaving, he turned to Anjali and said, "Thank you, Anjali Ji, for your help." He picked up the papers, gathered his bag, and left the room.

"Well played, Shankar," Anjali said as she returned to her chair. "But I do have one question."

"What's that?"

"You know that someone at your station is tipping off the dealers. What makes you believe Arvind's partners don't have an informant here, too? They are a connected bunch. I am sure you know that."

"I am placing my faith in you, Anjali Ji. I know you will carry out the investigation thoroughly, without bias or favour," Shankar asserted.

"And why is that?"

"Because I read up on you when I learned you were leading the narcotics case," Shankar responded.

"Then you must know that I've been transferred several times, have been at loggerheads with my bosses in many stations, and still haven't achieved the pay grade I deserve," Anjali contended.

"That's precisely why I think you won't let this go," Shankar said with a smile. "It has been my experience that the officers who stir the pot are the ones who get things done."

"Ha! It takes one to know one," Anjali said with a laugh.

"I wouldn't go that far. You have had far more success than me and solved more cases than I have. That's saying something, given that only two years of service separate us," Shankar added.

"And yet ..." Anjali sighed. She tilted her head, eyes fixed on the door. Then, she angled herself to face Shankar. "Your assistant seems uncomfortable with the idea of a woman officer."

Shankar smiled. "He will come around. Ashok is a good policeman. I am sure, in your career, you have dealt with many who looked at you differently."

"Oh! All the time," Anjali said with a grin. Then, she leaned forward. "You know, for a moment, I thought you trusted me because I am a woman police officer, and somehow, you thought women officers were less corruptible."

"Not at all, Anjali. If you must know, I see you as a good police officer who happens to be a woman. Nothing more, nothing less."

***

Shankar and Ashok sat at a table behind a shack on Versova Beach, blending in with the onlookers and beachgoers enjoying the warm weather.

"I never thought I'd find myself working in plain clothes

again," Ashok said, sipping his coconut water. "I feel kind of lost, to be honest, among such a relaxed crowd."

"Settle down, Ashok. We will be here for a while. It's a good old-fashioned stakeout, after all. We will be changing places now and then, but our focus is the back entrance over there," Shankar said, glancing toward the unloading area of the hotel.

"What precisely are we looking for, sir?"

"Do you remember our conversation about the lorries I spotted at the warehouse in Gurgaon?"

"Yes, sir." Ashok nodded, placing his hands on the table.

"And you have the numbers from the registration plates of those vehicles I saw that day, plus the ones we found on the ledgers in that warehouse?" Shankar continued.

"I do, sir, along with the ones from the trucking company, the vehicles our station used for our raids," Ashok said, reaching into his pocket.

Shankar stopped him. "Not now. Let's see what happens. If we spot a truck, we can check the numbers against those on your list."

"Right, sir," Ashok said. He sighed, gazing at the ocean beyond the beach, where a group of revellers blasted music beneath a coconut tree near the road. "You know, sir, when I joined the force, if someone would have told me that I'd be sitting in the library one day and then a couple of days later, spending a day at the beach for a stakeout while sipping coconut water, I'd have said they were crazy."

Shankar bit back a chuckle. "Don't worry, Ashok. You'll survive. Police work isn't always car chases and daring raids. Most of it is boring and mundane, like researching files or staking out locations for hours. Often, these are the tools we rely on to solve cases."

"I guess I am getting a taste of that, sir. Have you thought of how things would unfold if Gagan Ji and our superiors were to find out we lied to them about our purpose in Bombay?" Ashok asked thoughtfully. "I am worried about what will happen once they catch on."

"Don't fret about it. I will take the blame," Shankar said.

"Doesn't it bother you, sir?"

"Right now, no. I'll worry about it when the time comes. My main concern at the moment is uncovering the activities of this gang and finding out what happened to that little girl, Aria," Shankar said, keeping his eyes glued to the hotel's rear entrance.

"And her mother," Ashok added.

Shankar lowered his voice to a murmur. "Well, I do have to share something with you."

"What's that?"

"I had a long chat with one of my batchmates at the Jaipur station. On my request, he sent a constable to observe Dinesh's in-laws' address in Jaisalmer. As I expected, they located Aria's mother, Sanaya. But not the little girl," Shankar said.

"Oh! So, has Aria been kidnapped by this gang? Sanaya is in the Rajasthan Police, after all. Why didn't she go to the authorities with this?"

"I can't be sure, but I suspect this gang is using Aria as leverage to stop her mother from going to the police—or worse, forcing her to help them." Shankar drew a long breath.

"That's sad," Ashok mumbled.

"I also spoke to a few officers at the Jaisalmer station before leaving Delhi. I should be receiving an update later tonight. Once I have more details, I'll let you know what's happening." Shankar got up from the table to change locations.

For the next few hours, Shankar and Ashok took turns surveying the area around the building. It was a little after midnight when Shankar noticed a lorry rolling up to the back of the hotel. The driver and his companion got down and spoke to a guard, who jogged inside to fetch someone. As he waited, the driver looked around. Shankar gently tapped Ashok—who had nearly dozed off—and pointed to the lorry.

"Shh ..." Shankar put his index finger to his lips in a bid for silence. They ducked to keep out of sight, though Shankar knew the barrier beside the shack would provide ample cover in the dark. He peeked over the barrier to see the driver accompanying a smartly dressed gentleman into the back entrance. He couldn't make out the gentleman's face but saw enough to recognise the man from Nitya's photo. Nalin Kohli.

"What do we do now, sir?" whispered Ashok.

"I need you to read the license plate number of the lorry," Shankar responded. "Wait until a group of pedestrians are walking past, and stealthily join them. And please, Ashok. This time, we cannot raise any alarms."

"Don't worry, sir." Ashok sprang into action, creeping away and disappearing toward the beach. Shankar waited a few minutes and spotted him with a group of young backpackers. They strolled down the path adjacent to the curb where the lorry was parked. A few moments later, Ashok returned. He sat beside Shankar and yanked out a piece of paper from his pocket. Shankar kept his eyes trained on the truck while Ashok shone a tiny flashlight on the paper, comparing the digits scribbled on his palm with those on the list.

"Any luck?"

"Found it, sir," Ashok said, sounding confident. "It's one of the trucks from the warehouse in Gurgaon." He folded the paper, craned his neck, and raised his head to glimpse the lorry. "The back of the vehicle was firmly shut. I couldn't see what was inside."

"You will. We have to be patient," Shankar said.

Suddenly, there was a flurry of movement. The vehicle backed up toward the rear door, and the driver's companion opened the back of the truck. Shankar peered over the barrier to see a hotel employee go to a large switchboard near the wall and turn off all the lights. Shankar could barely see what was going on. The ambient light from the road and walkway was too dim to illuminate the lorry. From the shadows, Shankar heard footsteps tramping to and from the truck, and he strained his eyes to see what was going on.

"They are loading and unloading the cargo," Ashok mumbled. Shankar hushed him again, his heart dropping when he finally made out the cargo. As they looked on, Ashok gasped, his eyes gleaming with horror. "It's not drugs, artefacts, arms, or antiquities. We were wrong, sir. So very wrong." He sat beside Shankar, who remained standing, his eyes locked on the lorry. "What should we do now, sir? The two of us can't possibly raid the place. If we call for backup, the truck will be long gone when they arrive."

"I know," Shankar whispered as he sat back down beside Ashok. "I need to call Anjali and let her know what we found. We will give her the lorry number and ask her to relay the information to all the checkpoints leaving the city. If I am not mistaken, this lorry is one of several headed to Jaisalmer and across the border."

"Unbelievable," Ashok muttered, shaking his head. "Who would have thought ..."

"Ashok, pull yourself together. Our work here is done, but we must return to the Andheri Police Station ASAP, and I need to make a few calls."

"Yes, sir, but that ..." Ashok pointed toward the lorry.

"If we nab them now, they will warn all the others. We must cast a wider net and catch them in the act. Besides, these are low-level players. I suspect some of their bosses will be in Jaisalmer." Shankar clenched his hands into fists. "Time to go."

Leaving the beach, they drove straight to the Andheri Police Station, and after finishing there, Shankar and Ashok returned to the guesthouse. It was nearly five a.m. when they reached their rooms, and yet another long journey awaited them in a few hours. When Shankar's head hit the pillow, he tossed and turned, unable to sleep. He blinked his eyes open, spotting a few notes that were left on the bedside table. He reached over and picked them up. They were messages from people trying to get hold of him. Three messages were from Nitya, the last one having come in a couple of hours ago. He bolted upright, dialled the reception, and asked to be patched to Nitya's guesthouse. She picked up right away, and her words poured out before Shankar could say anything.

"Where have you been? I've been trying to reach you all day and into the night. No one seemed to know where you were and how to contact you," rambled Nitya.

"I am sorry, Nitya. I was at a stakeout. Please, calm down and tell me what happened. Is Kavita okay?"

"Yes, she is fine," Nitya said hurriedly.

"What is it, then?" Shankar asked. There was a pause on the other end of the line.

"I know what they are smuggling," she said. "It isn't drugs, weapons, or artefacts. They are smuggling people. The gang is involved in human trafficking."

"Yes, I know," Shankar confirmed.

"And there's something else," Nitya uttered, her voice wavering slightly.

"What is it, Nitya? You sound scared," Shankar said.

"You have probably suspected this as well, but this gang has infiltrated the state police and the local security agencies. There's no way they could pull this off and keep it quiet without involving other players in high places."

"It's a fair assumption, but as you know, I can't say one way or the other unless I know for certain." Shankar stroked his chin.

"And Shankar ..." Nitya cut herself short. A lengthy pause stretched between them, and he could hear Nitya taking quick, ragged breaths.

"What is it? There's something you're not telling me," Shankar pressed.

The deafening silence rang through the receiver before Nitya finally spoke.

"I recognised one of the people at that location. There was a tall gentleman who was marshalling folks at the ruins. Swati was right. It was the same man we saw on the train back from Bombay. He saw me today, and I am sure he recognised me. Now, he knows that I know who he is. And he knows what I was there for."

Blitz

Nitya paced up and down the hotel lobby in Jaisalmer as she waited for Shankar. The drive from Jodhpur had left her exhausted. She went to her room and tried to nap, but sleep wouldn't come. She couldn't stop calling the front desk every few minutes, asking whether Shankar had arrived or left a message. He hadn't. So, she gave up and parked herself at a patisserie near the reception, finding a nook from which she could see anyone entering or exiting the hotel.

A map sat folded on the table in front of her, alongside a cup of masala tea that she had hardly sipped and an open book she had barely read. She was tired of overhearing conversations from the other patrons about the sandstone architecture of this "Golden City" nestled in the heart of the Thar Desert. A photographer at the following table showed off pictures he had snapped of Jaisalmer Fort, a magnificent hilltop citadel that dominated the city's skyline.

After thirty minutes, which seemed like an eternity, Shankar walked in. Nitya jumped to her feet and ran up to him, directing him to a sofa at one corner of the lobby. Once they ordered a round of lassis, Nitya continued where she had left off the night before.

"Do you know if Nalin is heading back to Delhi?" she asked, not bothering with niceties.

"No. He will still be in Bombay or lying low at their hideout in Jaisalmer. Either way, he will be in our custody before the night's end, along with several other individuals we plan to apprehend here and in Bombay," Shankar added. "That's about as much as I can tell you now."

"I understand," Nitya said, crumpling her handkerchief.

"From everything you've dug up so far, I think you have plenty for a story," Shankar said.

"I do, and I'm planning to file the first of several reports starting tomorrow," Nitya confirmed. When she finally stopped to look at Shankar, she noticed his eyes drooping, dark bags hanging under them. "You must be tired. And I am guessing you still have a long night ahead."

Shankar smiled. "I'll rest better after tonight, but there is still much to do. I have asked Ashok and another officer to meet me here. They will be arriving in a few minutes. Is there something else you'd like to ask before they get here?"

"I heard from Swati about Dinesh Nath's body being discovered at the library," Nitya said. "I am guessing he found out about this gang."

Shankar nodded. "The investigation is underway, but yes, it's likely he either got caught up in all this, or he wanted to expose them, and that's what got him killed."

"And his wife and daughter?"

"That's what took me so long," Shankar started, then glanced at the waiter. The lassis arrived. After the waiter placed the tray on the table, Shankar picked up his glass and took several long sips, finishing almost half of it. Nitya smiled. Waving down the waiter, she asked him to fetch another glass and gently moved her lassi beside Shankar's.

"No, no, that's fine—"

"It's all right. You need this more than I do. Besides, I have ordered another one," Nitya said. "Now, about Dinesh's wife and daughter."

"Ashok and I met his wife earlier today. Although her parents are in Old Delhi, their ancestral home is in Jaisalmer. That's where she is holed up. She is distraught after hearing the news about Dinesh," Shankar uttered.

"And I am guessing she couldn't go to the police because this gang kidnapped her daughter," Nitya added.

Shankar nodded. "Aria."

"What?" Nitya asked, wrinkling her brow.

"Aria, that's her name. Dinesh and Sanaya's daughter."

"I see. I am assuming Sanaya has agreed to help you?" Nitya continued.

"Yes, but she is scared," Shankar said, taking another hearty swig from his glass.

"That's understandable."

"But yes, after hearing what they did to Dinesh, she told us everything she knows about the gang. The members, their hideouts—the works."

"That's good." As her lassi arrived, Nitya gave Shankar some time. He took a few deep breaths and moved on to the next glass. After a long gulp, he seemed calmer.

"Nitya, before you ask, you do realise that I won't be able to do what I did in Shimla," Shankar said, giving her a pointed look.

"What's that?" Nitya asked, though she knew full well where this was heading.

"I can't take you with me during the raids tonight," he continued. "I haven't even shared all the details with my department or the local police. No matter how things go, letting a journalist tag along will hardly look right."

"I know." Nitya nodded.

"And I cannot have you following us, either," Shankar added, his tone stern.

Nitya sighed. "I understand. I was going to suggest something else."

"Oh," Shankar said, straightening himself.

"I am guessing that, at some point during the night, you will be returning to the main police station with all your suspects," Nitya said.

"That's right."

"I was planning on being there when you arrived. I am sure you will make a statement for the press in the morning either way. If the press shows up at the station after everything is over, it shouldn't be a problem. Right?"

Shankar shook his head and smiled. "No, I suppose not. I am curious, though. As I mentioned before, you have everything you need for the story. Why wait until you see us arrive at the station? Even without tonight's operation, it's one hell of a conspiracy to report."

"Call me old-fashioned, Shankar. But I come from the school of journalism where accuracy is more important than speed," Nitya said before taking a drink of her lassi.

They chatted for a few more minutes before a woman officer and a constable stepped in, waving in their direction. Shankar waved back, got up, and led them to where Nitya was seated so they could introduce themselves. Ashok whispered something in Shankar's ear and left.

"I have read your articles," Anjali said. "I regularly look forward to your editorials. I have always enjoyed them."

"Thank you, ma'am," Nitya said with a smile.

"Oh, no need to 'ma'am' me. Just Anjali is fine. How do you know Shankar?"

"We go back a long way," Nitya responded. "He was a recruit posted in Callipur when I was working at a regional newspaper.

And now, of course, we're both in Delhi."

"We can sit and talk," Shankar said, pointing to the sofas.

"Oh, no. I am sure you have a lot to discuss, and throwing a journalist in the mix is never a good idea," Nitya stated, and they all laughed. "Before I go, I have a question for you, Shankar." Nitya angled toward him.

"What's that?"

"Knowing what we know about this human trafficking operation, it is not too far-fetched to assume there are people involved in other organisations, including the police." Nitya gauged his reaction.

Shankar just shrugged. "Everything we know so far does point to insiders, informers, and players at all levels, but I won't confirm a thing until the investigation is complete," he noted. "We have to snuff out every last one. I suspect tonight is just the beginning of a long investigation."

"I understand. But if indeed they have their tentacles everywhere, they must have some appendages in the local police, too. How did you convince the force here to undertake what will certainly be a large raid at such short notice?" Nitya could see Anjali suppressing a smile from the corner of her eye, but she kept her gaze locked on Shankar.

"I can't get into all the details, Nitya. But the gang made one cardinal mistake that most criminals, even professional gangs, don't make," Shankar said.

Nitya arched an eyebrow. "What's that?"

"They went after a policeman, or in this case, a policewoman—one of our own," Shankar responded.

"You mean Sanaya."

"That's right. She is a constable and a member of the Rajasthan Police. They hounded her, killed her husband, and kidnapped their daughter. No matter what colours you wear, any force will close ranks when that happens," Shankar declared.

Nitya hummed in thought, not entirely convinced by that explanation. But she decided to let it go. "All right, I'll leave you officers to it, then. Please be safe. With any luck, I will see you again tonight at the police station following a successful operation."

"Thank you," Shankar said, and Anjali nodded. Nitya left them in the lobby and returned to her room to call Swati.

***

Sitting down on the sofas in the corner of the lobby, Shankar and Anjali promptly ordered some tea and pakoras and then got down to business. Shankar cracked open a file, glancing around for prying eyes. Satisfied, he pulled out a map and unfolded it on the coffee table. Anjali started speaking before he could lay out the plan.

"Hobnobbing with a journalist might get you into trouble," Anjali remarked.

"True, but I trust Nitya. She is a good friend and shared some details with me that aided my investigation." Shankar kept his eyes on the map.

"Wasn't she the one who wrote that article on the police's heavy-handedness during the protests at India Gate, the one that landed you in hot water? If I recall, that's why you ended up posted in that awful station in Old Delhi," Anjali continued, narrowing her eyes.

"I am happy you've done your homework," Shankar said, holding back a smile. "If you must know, it's true, that operation didn't pan out as expected. But I was more disappointed with my top brass, who were more interested in finding a scapegoat than figuring out what happened."

"But the press got after you," Anjali said.

"They did. However, they were only doing their job. And in hindsight, that posting in Old Delhi led to my investigation of the riots in the walled city. That eventually helped me get a promotion and a better posting," Shankar remarked.

"And what you told her about the police closing ranks—not entirely true, is it?"

Shankar grinned. "Not entirely, no. It did help, however, in getting the local officers worked up about tonight's raid."

"There's still a chance that someone on the gang's payroll will warn them." Anjali folded her arms over her chest.

Shankar nodded. "I have thought of that, and that's why—"

"How much does Nitya know of tonight's raids?" Anjali blurted.

"She is completely in the dark. I haven't shared the details with anyone. That's why I need to speak with you," Shankar said, putting his index finger on the map.

"What am I looking at?" Anjali reached into her purse to bring out her glasses. Putting them on, she pored over the large map of Jaisalmer and the surrounding areas. Her eyes lingered on the blue dot north of the city and a red mark on the outskirts, somewhere in the desert.

"This," Shankar said, placing his finger on the blue dot, "is where everyone thinks the raid will be conducted. It is an old, abandoned warehouse that was used for storing car parts and other metals. As far as everyone knows, that's our main target."

Anjali pointed to the red mark on the map. "And this one?"

"That"—Shankar nodded at Anjali—"is where we are actually going. It is four kilometres from the other warehouse, on the same highway."

"What exactly will we find there?"

"The gang's main hideout, a remote compound with a few scattered buildings. The compound used to be an old mill that has since closed. There is a large shed and two buildings, and it's located near a village," Shankar added, pointing to the name on the map.

"And how certain are we that the gang will be there?"

"I am confident we will find not only gang members but some of their bosses as well. We'll also uncover the route they take through the desert to cross the border while evading the military," Shankar said, then paused. Footsteps sounded behind him, and he quickly folded the map. A waiter arrived to serve them their tea, leaving a plate of pakoras on the table.

Anjali took a few sips and then looked at Shankar pensively. "So, that's how you are making sure the raid is a success. Even if there's a leak at the local station, they will only know about the dummy location, not our target."

"Right," Shankar confirmed.

"And when will you tell them of the true destination?"

"When we are approaching the false one. You saw the map—it's on the same highway. We will be in the lead Jeep, and I will tell the driver to keep going until we reach the actual hideout," Shankar responded.

"It's quite a plan, Shankar. I am impressed," Anjali said. "How many people know about this?"

"Me, you, and Ashok."

"I guess you learned your lesson from the raids in Delhi."

"Ah, about that. We are also trying to smoke out some folks there," Shankar continued.

"How?" Anjali took off her glasses.

"Someone at our station has been informing the gang of

our raids. Tonight, there is another raid planned in Delhi at a warehouse that we suspect is being used for trafficking." Shankar explained how they had identified the constable who'd been calling the toll booth number and informing a contact there of the raids.

"So, this constable will call the toll booth number. Once he tells the shop owner who he wants to talk to, presumably, someone will fetch him. Then, you will nab him red-handed," Anjali summarised.

"That's right." Shankar nodded. "Someone will be waiting at the phone booth, and yes, a trap has been laid to catch the folks involved."

"And what makes you so certain there aren't other people in your station who are in on this besides the constable?"

"I am not. That's why I have requested an officer from another station to look into this," Shankar went on.

"Are your superiors aware?" Anjali prodded.

"I have informed them, vaguely, that I am looking into a mole in our station without giving out too many details or sharing the plan," Shankar muttered.

"This could go horribly wrong for you, Shankar. I hope you know that," Anjali said, wrinkling her forehead.

"I know, but I couldn't think of any other way. I didn't want to take any chances tonight. Speaking of which, there's another thing I need to tell you," Shankar said, picking up a pakora.

"What's that?"

"I had a long discussion with the commander of the Border Security Force, which has a contingent further out. They have agreed to block the highway beyond our destination in case anyone escapes our clutches."

"Have you shared the hideout location with them?"

"No," Shankar replied, shaking his head.

"How did you get them to agree without engaging your superiors?"

"I informed them that a gang has been operating in the region, smuggling men, women, and children back and forth across the border right under their noses. I told the commander his help would be critical in capturing the gang and uncovering the route. If we succeed tonight, BSF can take credit as part of the operation," Shankar said.

"And if we don't succeed?"

"Then he doesn't have to say anything. If it all goes south, he can point the finger at me."

"You are playing a dicey game here, Shankar." Anjali locked eyes with him. "If things don't go as planned, you risk being suspended, considering all the folks you have hoodwinked. And if things go well, chances are you will be applauded but also reprimanded for the means you employed. You realise that, don't you?"

Shankar nodded. "Like I said, I couldn't think of any other way. I was asked not to prioritise this, but I only got approval to travel to Bombay and Rajasthan on the pretext of an unrelated case. I have become sick and tired of carrying out raids only to come up empty-handed. This is the best I could do under the circumstances."

Anjali scooted closer to Shankar. "I know, Shankar. It bothers me that you had to do all this to get here. You shouldn't have had to."

Shankar smiled. "Well, all's not lost. We still have folks in the force who want to do the right thing. When I spoke at the local station earlier today, I was thrilled to see so many people ready to help. A few bad apples shouldn't deter us from pursuing what's right."

"I agree, they shouldn't." Anjali nodded. "You know, my husband works in the private sector. He's never understood the pressures and political hoop-jumping in our organisation. He wonders, at times, whether I enjoy my job. And trust me when I say that being a woman makes it much harder."

"I can't say I understand. I have never faced that particular bias, but you are right. It is difficult to talk about this with anyone from the outside," Shankar said, thinking back on his long career.

"What I wanted to say was that people like you and Ashok, and some others that I have encountered, make it worthwhile," Anjali said, smiling.

"Hopefully, all will go well tonight. Then, freeing those people from this modern-day form of slavery will also make it worthwhile," Shankar added.

"What does success look like for you tonight? What will make you happy?"

"Apprehending the gang members and affiliates at the hideout, uncovering the route used for smuggling, and freeing the people being held captive constitute success in my mind," Shankar replied. "Returning Aria to her mother, Sanaya would make me happy."

Before they could continue, Ashok marched into the lobby and announced that they were ready at the station. Sharing a glance, Shankar and Anjali got up, and once they reached the station, they declared to their peers that they would be heading out after nightfall.

***

It was ten p.m. when Shankar's Jeep raced past the location of the blue dot on the map, barreling toward their actual destination. Anjali and Ashok, sitting behind the driver, and Shankar all smiled. They glanced back through the rear windshield to see the convoy of Jeeps and police vans still following them. Once they reached the compound, Shankar hopped out of the vehicle and barked out orders to surround the area.

They had stopped a mile from their destination, and Shankar asked all drivers to shut off their engines and ordered that no one shine their flashlights. The only ambient light was from the moon and stars bearing down on the sandy desert. The darkness and vast stretches of rolling white sand dunes provided ample cover for Shankar and his party to approach unnoticed. There were a few surprised looks among the police party, but they were too preoccupied with following orders to ask questions.

Anjali positioned herself to lead the charge with her contingent from the main gate while Shankar and Ashok focused on the back entrance. The entire compound was encased behind high walls, and another group of policemen ensured no one escaped by scaling them. Then, two large police vans drove up to the gates at each entrance to block any vehicle from exiting.

As they drew near, Shankar looked around. The two sentries manning each entrance were too busy listening to their transistors to notice them. He knew that no one was expecting company, and the element of surprise was critical for his plan to work.

"All right, time to get the trucks in place," Shankar said, turning to Ashok. The constable nodded and whispered something into the police two-way radio. Within sixty seconds, Ashok's party crouched behind a dune facing the back entrance and saw a slow-moving police van. With its lights off, the vehicle rolled up to block the exit. The driver tried his best, but the noise of the van's engine alerted the men guarding the gate.

Shankar watched from his hiding place. Two guards from the compound approached the driver. At the same time, constables poured out from the back of the van, tiptoeing toward the front of the vehicle. The first guard started shouting at the driver, but he was immediately silenced with a blow to the gut. The other guard yelled at the top of his lungs, swinging around to scramble back to the compound. But it was too late. Another constable hauled him back and overpowered him.

"Should we go now, sir?" Ashok fidgeted with his rifle.

"No, wait!" Shankar ordered. "Let's be careful with our weapons. There are people in there we are trying to save. Remember that."

The lights in the compound flickered on, followed by the roar of vehicles from the other side of the wall. Anjali's voice came through the radio. They had completely blocked the front entrance, dealt with the guards, and waited for Shankar's instructions. Shankar glanced at the wide-open gates of the back entrance. He could see two cars trying to make a run for it through the front gate, but Anjali's party blocked them. It was what he saw next that made his stomach drop. The headlights from the police van shone on a group of children in tattered clothes bound in chains in the middle of the courtyard. Before Shankar could give his order, Ashok flew to his feet.

"Enough of this nonsense. It's time to go!" he bellowed. Ashok's speed took Shankar by surprise. He was already halfway through the gates, his rifle blazing at the gang members who were trying to flee. Shankar and the rest followed him inside. The element of surprise had worked better than expected.

"Here!" Anjali shouted from her position near the front gate as she marshalled her contingent, rounding up the miscreants and their weapons. Shankar's eyes fell on the victims. Men, women, and children huddled together, shivering in the cold night. Heavy chains and thick ropes bound them to one another. Shankar quickly ordered two constables to free them and bring them some of the water and food they were carrying in the minivans.

The sight of the prisoners quivering in the cold night, chained in the middle of the courtyard, pierced his heart. Their awful plight prompted some constables to dole out more force on their captors than was needed. As he drew closer, he recognised one of the young girls from her photograph. It was Dinesh and Sanaya's daughter, Aria. Shankar breathed a sigh, relieved she was alive and well. After a while, Shankar ordered that all the gang members be handcuffed and thrown into the police vans.

"We are not done yet," Shankar said, turning to Anjali, who had walked up next to him.

"What do you mean?"

"Stay alert. We have to search these buildings, floor by floor, room by room," Shankar went on, drawing his revolver. "I saw some flashlights on the upper floors," he added, pointing to the blocks.

"Right," Anjali hissed. "I will take that one." She motioned to the building closest to her. Waving down her contingent, she barked orders to surround the building before switching on a large flashlight and leading a few constables through the main door.

"What's going on here, sir?"

Shankar turned to see his assistant jogging up beside him.

"We have missed a few," Shankar said, pointing to the second building.

"I've got this, sir," Ashok said, lifting his rifle and gesturing to some constables nearby to join him.

"No, Ashok. Please stay here to ensure all the victims are accounted for, and get them some blankets. I will take care of this." Gathering a few constables, Shankar slowly led the group through the main door of the other building. They crept up the stairs to search for any remaining gang members.

It was only when they reached the top floor, near the doorway to a large room, that they were met with a hail of bullets. Shankar ordered everyone to the ground, then yelled to the gang members that they were surrounded and should surrender. It didn't have the desired effect. A few beats of silence passed before a new slew of gunshots rang out. He turned to the nearest constable, who waited in the stairwell.

"I need you to go back down and climb the ladder on the opposite side." He pointed to the smaller room on the same floor they had already searched. "Make sure the door to the roof is locked. Take a few constables up and wait if anyone breaks through the door. But before that, send Ashok upstairs with some smoke bombs and grenades."

"Yes, sir," came the reply. The constable's footsteps hurried down the stairs. Ashok crouched beside Shankar with a bag in hand a few minutes later.

"How many do you need, sir?"

"Let's start with the smoke bombs. Give me two. That should be enough to snuff them out," Shankar said.

Once he tossed them, smoke engulfed the room, and three teary-eyed men came rushing out, coughing and choking, right into the clutches of Shankar's men. Another one jumped out the window and landed on the ground with a loud thud. Within seconds, he was screaming in pain, probably from a few broken limbs. The last one dashed up the stairwell and managed to break down the door, only to be welcomed into the waiting arms and handcuffs of the constables stationed there. When Shankar returned down the stairs, Anjali was waiting with a map. As he approached, he saw a red mark on her cheek and a gash on her forehead.

"Look what I found," Anjali said with a smirk. She held up the folded document, seemingly oblivious to the fact that she was bleeding.

"Are you all right?" Shankar asked, rushing over to her.

"Never mind that. I am fine. Look at this, Shankar." She unfolded the map and then shone her flashlight on it.

"Oh my God, that's the smuggling route!" Shankar stated, his heart pounding.

"Yes! This is the path they were using to travel back and forth over the border."

"Great work, Anjali. But you need to get that checked out," Shankar said, pointing to her forehead.

"I am fine. And yes, I will. Don't worry!" Her smile never wavered. Leaning in, she continued, "Two people were hiding in one of the rooms. I think they are among the bosses. If we interrogate them, alongside the ones you nabbed from your building and all the others we captured tonight, we should also be able to track down some masterminds."

Shankar nodded. "This went better than I expected. Apart from you, was anyone injured in your party?"

"A few scrapes and bruises, Shankar. Don't fuss about it. Just look at the faces of the constables and officers who are here. They are ecstatic," Anjali exclaimed. "You should be, too."

"I am," Shankar said in a more sombre tone, gazing at the van that held the victims.

Anjali stepped closer. "What is it?"

"What an ordeal they must have suffered," Shankar breathed, glancing at the rugged, tired faces of the victims.

"Yes," sighed Anjali. "Did we find Aria?"

"Yes, I recognised her among that group in the courtyard," Shankar replied, which made Anjali smile. Before he could say more, Ashok walked up to them and declared that all the victims and gang members were now ready to be transported to the station. Shankar turned, summoned a local officer, and instructed him to stay with a large contingent in the compound and cordon it off. Bringing another officer aside, Shankar directed him to contact a forensics team and remain alert. When he turned back to Anjali, she watched Ashok shuffling back to the Jeep while holding Aria's hand.

"I heard he led quite a charge today," Anjali said, motioning to Ashok. "It seems Aria is in good hands." She beamed as Ashok gently hoisted the little girl into the Jeep and placed her between him and the driver.

"He did, and it surprised everyone," Shankar said.

"It was either an act of incredible foolishness or remarkable bravery."

"Both, and they often are," Shankar said with a smile.

Anjali nodded. "Back to the station now?"

"Yes," Shankar said, and together, they walked back to their Jeep.

***

It was nearly four a.m. when Nitya spotted the headlights of Shankar's Jeep and the rest of his convoy returning to the station. She had almost dozed off, seated at a roadside dhaba across from the main gate of the Jaisalmer Police Station. The sputtering engines of the police Jeeps and vans first awakened her. Only a few people were on the street at this time, including a young woman outside the gates who was pacing anxiously.

Everyone seemed surprised when the large police convoy rolled in. As she got up, she noticed a few officers and constables helping the occupants of the first two vans down and carefully herding them into the main building. The treatment being meted out to the ones in the following two vans was not so gentle. As they got down, one by one, they were all in handcuffs and chains. A few of them wore dirty but expensive-looking attire. The constables accompanying them hurled obscenities and dragged them violently into the police compound.

What Nitya saw next made her shudder. A tall man in handcuffs, a bruise on his cheek, was being dragged out of the van and shoved through the gates of the station. It was the same man she had seen at Kangra Mahal in Jodhpur, the one she and Swati had encountered on the train back to Delhi from Bombay. A few seconds later, her eyes fell on Nalin. He looked different. His eyes were downcast, tears streaming down his cheeks as he shook his head.

After a few minutes, Shankar stepped out. He was in deep conversation with Anjali. She waved when they glanced in her direction, and they both waved back. Shankar then murmured something to Anjali, pointing her to an ambulance parked on the other side of the street. Next, he walked over to Ashok. That's when Nitya saw the little girl. Shankar kneeled and whispered something in the girl's ear, making her smile. He took her hand and guided her past the vans and Jeeps toward the woman flitting frantically from one vehicle to the other. Then, they stopped.

For a moment, time stood still. The woman shuffled up to Shankar and locked eyes with the little girl. The little girl then released Shankar's hand and ran to the woman, jumping into her open arms and hugging her tightly. Nitya turned her gaze to Shankar, noticing a smile on his face as he looked on. The woman was still sobbing, clutching the little girl in her arms and kissing her cheeks.

Shankar spent a few more minutes talking to another officer before crossing the street to meet Nitya.

"Is that ...?" Nitya pointed to the little girl who was still wrapped in the woman's arms.

"Yes, that's Aria and her mother, Sanaya," Shankar whispered. "God only knows what they went through. And now, she has to tell the little girl about her father."

"I can't imagine their ordeal," Nitya said, pausing momentarily. "How did it go?"

"Better than expected," Shankar said. His words were chipper, but Nitya could sense the exhaustion in his voice. His uniform was covered in black soot, his hair was unkempt, and his face drooped.

"I'm glad. I saw those people in the first two vans. Some of them were just kids, small children," Nitya noted.

"Yes," Shankar said feebly.

"Were you able to apprehend everyone? I hope no one got hurt."

"We captured everyone who was there. We need to question them to see where that leads," Shankar added. "And no, there were no injuries. A few scrapes and bruises, but nothing serious."

"That's good," Nitya said as she scooted closer to Shankar.

He smiled. Even the dark lines on his face and his bloodshot eyes couldn't contain how pleased he was. "Aria is safe, and she's back where she belongs."

"Wonderful. I'm guessing it will be a while before all the victims are placed back in their homes since they'll need to be questioned first," Nitya continued.

"I will hang around the station for the next few days to make sure of that. I need to talk to them and find out how they were enticed and kidnapped. Some preliminary questioning revealed that the gang was using a fake adoption agency, but I don't have all the details yet." He gave her a pointed look. "This is just for your information, not the papers."

"I understand." Nitya nodded. Noting that Shankar's legs had started shaking, she swooped in to grab him by his shoulders and then dragged him into a chair. She turned to the dhaba owner and ordered some water. "You need to rest, Shankar."

"I know," he said, smiling weakly. He gulped down the water that a waiter brought him and then leaned back into his chair. "This is just the beginning," Shankar continued, gesturing to the station across the street.

"I am guessing this will lead to other investigations, more raids and arrests, and hopefully some accolades for you," Nitya remarked.

"We will see. People who do this kind of thing have friends in high places. But yes, this is big. They won't manage to sweep this under the rug," Shankar said thoughtfully.

"And what about you?"

"Oh, given the scale of this operation and the arrests we've been making, I'm sure that things will look good in the short term," Shankar mumbled, though a shadow fell over his face.

"And in the long term ...?"

"When the dust settles, we'll see how the chips fall. I am sure I will get some verbal reprimand for keeping my superiors in the dark," Shankar noted.

"I would think this is big enough for the ends to justify the means," Nitya declared.

"We will see," Shankar said. "There is something else I need to tell you."

"What?"

"Several raids were carried out tonight, spanning multiple locations. The details will be in the press communication tomorrow morning. One of the targets was the hotel where Kavita and Nalin work. Due to Kavita's relationship with Nalin, we will need a statement from her at some point," Shankar said.

"Of course," sighed Nitya. "Kavita and I guessed as much. We figured that if indeed Nalin was involved, she would be questioned. She will share everything she knows."

"I don't want you to worry," Shankar said quickly. "We are dealing with a professional gang that has hoodwinked and cheated many people."

Nitya stared at the table. "I did confront Kavita, you know. You'd think she would suspect something, working in the same hotel and spending so much time with Nalin," she whispered.

"It's not her fault. Falling in love with the wrong person is never a crime. If one were guilty of that, then ..." Shankar stopped and smiled.

"Well," Nitya said, looking at Shankar, "I will be sure to tell her you said that."

"You can also tell her that we wouldn't have busted this gang without her wonderful sister's help," Shankar added with a twinkle.

"Ha! That's a bit much. You were already on to Dinesh's disappearance before I said a word," Nitya remarked.

"True, but the piece of the puzzle we were missing was the connection between Arvind Kapoor and Nalin Kohli. That came from you."

"So, Arvind was involved after all?"

"That is still under investigation, but it seems unlikely that Arvind knew of all the nefarious activities his partners and Nalin were up to. When he did find out, he had a falling out with his partners, probably angry that all this had been going on under his nose. He threatened to go to the police, which did him in. Again, all off the record, Nitya," Shankar warned.

"Yes, of course. Wow," Nitya muttered.

"And you already know about Dinesh. What you probably don't know is that—"

"—the gang was using the library to connect buyers and sellers. Dinesh found that out while working at the library, and they killed him for it," Nitya said, finishing Shankar's sentence.

Shankar blinked back, his eyes widening. "How on earth did you know that? I never told you—"

"You know, journalists have been known to spend time in the library too. It's not just cops," Nitya said, to which Shankar gave her a big smile.

"Impressive, Nitya, really impressive," Shankar said. "Do you know how the gang found out about Dinesh?"

"On that, I am not sure. Was it Nalin? He was the only one who could have connected him," Nitya said.

Shankar nodded. "Dinesh rented the apartment from Bharat and tried to hide Aria there for a while, but I am guessing that at some point, Nalin visited the library for gang-related activities and found Dinesh working there. Of course, he may have also known that Dinesh worked in the warehouse. I am not sure. But he certainly didn't know where he lived. There must have been some confrontation or altercation during which Dinesh threatened to go to the police. The gang also knew that Sanaya was a policewoman. They kidnapped Aria to keep her quiet after dealing with Dinesh."

"What a mess," Nitya mumbled. "At least Aria is back with Sanaya, and of course, those other poor souls are safe too."

"Yes, just like Aria, the children are all orphans. I suspect the gang created a fake agency that took them in and sold them to the highest bidders in India and abroad."

"That's just awful! It's disgusting, harrowing." Nitya shook her head vigorously, anger boiling up inside her. "I hope these fellows burn in hell!" They sat silently for a few minutes before Nitya continued, "I wanted to ask you one thing that has been on my mind."

"What's that?"

"When did you first begin to suspect that it wasn't drugs, antiquities, or arms that they were smuggling?"

Shankar took a deep breath. "At every warehouse we went to, I found coat hangers with remnants of clothes—jackets and pants of different sizes. That didn't make sense. Then, the photos were swapped at the library. Why would anyone swap pictures of drugs? Antiquities or weapons, perhaps. I ruled out drugs when no one objected to me travelling to Shimla, Bombay, and Rajasthan for my narcotics case. They already had that covered. Antiquities made some sense. They could be hidden in air coolers. But that didn't explain the clothes and the hangers. Something didn't seem right. The final piece locked into place when I saw what happened at the Versova Beach Hotel in Bombay. That's when I realised they were trafficking humans."

"And the air coolers?" Nitya asked.

"They are large enough to hold kids, and the crates for the taller ones," Shankar said solemnly.

"God, Shankar! How long has this been going on?"

Shankar shrugged. "We will find out once we start interrogating that lot," he said, pointing to the police station.

As Nitya thought this all over, the waiter came by with another water bottle and asked if they wanted snacks or tea. They refused, and Nitya asked for the bill. "What's next for you?" Shankar asked.

"I am heading back to Delhi today, where I'll file the story for tomorrow morning's paper," Nitya replied.

"It's a big one for you—not that you need it. You have been a star reporter ever since you started," Shankar said.

"Ha! Hardly. We will see how things go," Nitya sighed.

"Are you still worried about what will happen if the owners' relatives get caught up?" Shankar asked. "I am sure you found the link, right?"

Nitya nodded. "I will do what I must. And as a good friend said, we will wait and see how the chips fall once the dust settles," she declared, and they laughed.

"All right. I must head back to the station," Shankar said, getting up with some effort.

Nitya settled the bill and followed suit. Before Shankar could turn to leave, she touched his arm and looked him in the eye. "You need to take care of yourself, Shankar. Eat, sleep, rest—and all the other things one should do, but they neglect because they get caught up at work."

"I know," Shankar said with a nod, "and I will."

"I'll see you in a few days in Delhi, then?" Nitya asked as they exited the dhaba.

"Yes, and I look forward to reading tomorrow's paper." Shankar shot her a grin. "*The Daily Citizen News.*" Nitya smiled. After watching him leave, she turned around and headed to her car.

Mask

Winter turned into spring, and the arrival of Holi signalled a change from bitter cold to warmer, brighter days. A lot had happened in the two months since Nitya returned from Jaisalmer, and she was ready to start a new chapter in her life. As she stepped into the living room, she heard Kavita listening to ghazals in her bedroom. It was early for her to be up, especially on a Sunday morning, but Nitya was happy that her sister was slowly putting her past with Nalin behind her. Nitya placed the two cups of coffee on the table with a plate of biscuits.

"When are you meeting him?" Kavita asked, joining her in the living room.

"In a couple of hours."

"A bit early for a Sunday lunch, isn't it?" Scooting closer to her sister, Kavita propped her feet on Nitya's lap and rested her head on the cushions.

"It's a new thing nowadays—they are calling it brunch. I figured you, being younger, would know about it," Nitya said as she bit into a biscuit.

"Ha! So, are you going to tell him?"

"You mean about London? Of course," Nitya replied.

"Well, that too. But that's not what I was asking," Kavita said. Nitya knew exactly what Kavita was asking but didn't want to discuss it.

"What, then?" Nitya asked with a mischievous smile.

"I am talking about how you are now done and dusted with

the professor, and you have moved on," Kavita started. She sat up slightly before adding a more direct tone, "and that you are interested in him."

"Stop it," Nitya snapped, feigning annoyance and playfully tapping Kavita on her knee.

"Honestly, what exactly are you waiting for? You have known Shankar for more than ten years now. You like him; he likes you. I think it's time you gave it a go," Kavita stated.

"For one, he is still married," Nitya started, but Kavita cut her off before she could finish.

"They have been separated for years and don't even live together. Her life is with their son in Mussoorie, and he is here in Delhi, all alone, unattached."

"Okay, okay. I get it, but ..."

"But what?"

"I don't know. What if he's not interested?" Nitya asked, her chest constricting as she stared at the wall.

"Believe me, he is interested. You told me that each time you meet, you talk forever and enjoy each other's company. But you know Shankar better than I do. Do you think he would do that with someone he didn't like?"

Nitya kept quiet. "If he says no ..."

"He won't. Besides, you won't know how he feels unless you ask him!" Kavita pressed.

"If he was interested, he would have said something by now, don't you think?"

Kavita drilled Nitya with a reprimanding stare. "You know, for someone who touts herself as a modern, liberal-minded woman, I'm surprised you don't walk the talk when it comes to your feelings."

"I know what you are saying, Kavita. It's just that ... if he turns me down, or if things don't work out, it will be awkward between us. I fear I'd lose a good friend."

Kavita sat upright and wrapped her arms around Nitya. "That's a risk we all take when we put our hearts on the line, isn't it? I should know. I have already had a failed marriage and an ex-boyfriend who turned out to be roped up in a human trafficking gang. I just know that Shankar is right for you, and you are right for him. I will be damned if I don't force, harass, and plead with my sister to give it a go."

Nitya smiled. "All right."

"All right, what?" Kavita nearly shouted, her eyes flying wide.

"I can't make any promises, but I will see how things go during our brunch, and then ..."

"Then you'll tell him that you are in love with him and want to have lots and lots of babies with him!" Kavita blurted, laughing loudly and snapping her fingers. Nitya tried to grab her by the shoulders playfully, but Kavita managed to wiggle out of her grasp and run away.

"Just wait, Missy. Wait until I get back. I am not done with you yet!" yelled Nitya.

***

The Sunday crowd was sparse in the upscale Central Delhi restaurant where Nitya had agreed to meet Shankar. It was Nitya who arrived first, and she asked for a booth on the first floor overlooking the sprawling Lodi Gardens. She couldn't recall the last time she arrived early to a rendezvous with Shankar. He always showed up first. While waiting, she gazed out the large windows and saw families with children playing in the gardens alongside some old men and women doing yoga. As she watched the peaceful scene, she mentally played out her conversation with Kavita earlier. A familiar voice from across the restaurant pulled her out of her thoughts.

"Nitya!" Shankar roared, rushing to the booth and sitting across from her. He looked different—more relaxed—and a bit older without his uniform.

"Happy belated Holi. It is always nice to see you. I'm glad you could make it," Nitya gushed. "I do have something to discuss with you. And don't worry, it's not about a case, story, or any sort of trouble."

"I am glad to hear that," Shankar said as the waiter arrived to take their order.

They quickly ordered omelettes, tikka, bread, and juice before diving into what had happened in the two months since they'd last seen one another. Nitya was guarded in her responses, and she wondered if Shankar noticed. Usually, she would be far more cheerful and playful, but she was still wrestling with whether to admit her feelings to Shankar. As for Shankar, he was his usual self, switching from cricket to music to Bollywood and finally to the case that had brought them together once again.

"How is Kavita? Has she managed to put this whole thing with Nalin behind her?"

Nitya breathed a shallow sigh. "Not entirely, but I think the initial shock has passed. She felt betrayed, and getting over that will take a while. The good news is, things are getting better, and she is happier now."

"That's good. I'm glad and hope she can move on," Shankar said. "I wish things were that simple on our end with the investigation."

"Oh! Are more people going to be implicated?"

"Perhaps, but the main players linked to this case are all

accounted for—you know them already. Now, it's up to the courts. And as you know, things there can be unpredictable," Shankar said, straightening his back when their food arrived. After taking a few bites, he continued. "I am glad we could sniff out the culprits in our station. I suspect more are lurking elsewhere, and we didn't nab all the masterminds, but at least they are scared, and the press is on to them."

"True," mumbled Nitya, chewing her food quickly.

"Speaking of the press, I haven't seen your columns in the paper lately. What's going on?" Shankar asked, putting down his knife and fork as he waited.

Nitya smiled. Glancing up at Shankar, she put down her fork. "I am no longer working with *The Daily Citizen News*."

"What?" Shankar blurted, which drew a few curious stares. He glanced at the other patrons, smiled apologetically, and turned his gaze back to Nitya. "What happened? Did you quit?"

"Not quite," Nitya said softly.

"Oh my God! You were let go."

Nitya nodded. "Well, it was only a matter of time after ..."

"After the Thapars' in-laws ended up on the list of the accused," Shankar said, shaking his head. "It shouldn't have come to this. I mean, you had to write the story and report what you uncovered. What else were they expecting?"

"Well, I did manage to do that. But it didn't go down well with my bosses and the owners. When the dust settled, they decided to—"

"That's so unfair. Aren't you angry about this? Hurt?" Shankar asked.

"I was, for a while, but then I realised it was always going to happen. I knew what the aftermath would be," Nitya declared.

"But it was such a good article. That exclusive scoop must

have increased circulation. If they are so fixated on that, this must have helped their bottom line."

"It probably did. I don't know," Nitya mumbled.

"Why wasn't there a big fuss made over this? It was a terrific story, a big conspiracy that was unearthed. I am surprised other papers didn't pick up on it," Shankar said in an indignant tone, convincing Nitya that he was genuinely upset and concerned. That brought a swell of warmth to her chest.

"Do you know the shelf life of a scandal or a good story?" Nitya asked, picking up her fork again.

"No," Shankar muttered.

"Till the next one, and in this city, in this country, there is no shortage of scandals," Nitya said and smiled. "Truthfully, this paper was not the right fit for me. At some point, we would have parted ways, but it would have been easier, professionally, if I'd left under different circumstances."

"Still ... And why didn't you tell me about this?" Shankar demanded.

"I wanted to tell you in person," Nitya responded.

He breathed a long sigh, "What will you do now? I am sure, with your years of experience and strong reputation, you will find something quickly, something you want."

"Well, there is some news on that front as well," Nitya said, wiping her mouth with a napkin and leaning back in her chair.

"Oh! You are full of surprises today," Shankar said.

"That's what happens when we go without seeing each other for this long."

"Well, we ought to do something about that," Shankar said. Then, he called for the waiter and turned to Nitya. "Do you want tea or coffee?"

"Tea for me, please," Nitya responded.

Shankar quickly ordered a teapot and continued, "All right, let's have it. What's your next adventure?"

"I can't tell you the paper's name because I still have to sign the final offer and confidentiality agreements. But I promise I won't keep it from you. A paper in London wants me to be their foreign correspondent in India," Nitya said.

"Wow! That's wonderful. Which one is it? *Times, Express, Telegraph*?" Shankar demanded, leaning forward.

Nitya smiled, then shrugged.

"Oh, come on." Shankar let out a small huff. "All right. I understand you can't tell me ..."

"Shankar, no one knows about this. Even my parents and Kavita only found out because my pesky little sister opens all my mail. But I'll let you know next week," Nitya said.

"That's all right. I am happy for you, Nitya." He cast her a warm smile. "So, when do you start if this all works out?"

"They want me to go to London for six months for a training program in which all their foreign correspondents participate. Then, I will be posted in Delhi or Bombay," Nitya responded.

"That's wonderful. I am sure you will love it. They are lucky to have you."

Nitya grinned. "It's always good to have someone like you in my corner."

"That's what friends are for," Shankar said. The waiter arrived with their tea, and Nitya kept her eyes on Shankar as the man poured the steaming beverage into their cups and left.

"What about you, Shankar? Your bosses must be happy with how things turned out, with you busting a human trafficking ring." Nitya sighed. "What's the world coming to, Shankar? I mean, smuggling kids? Things like this make you realise what an awful lot we sometimes deal with."

"True. Something like this can take its toll and be draining," Shankar agreed.

"And disheartening, seeing what fellow humans can do to one another," Nitya added.

Shankar nodded.

"Of course, you probably see this sort of thing a lot more than I do. I am surprised it doesn't get to you."

"It does, but I see other things too," Shankar added.

"Like what?"

"I saw Dinesh Nath, a young man from a modest background, coming to do the right thing, wanting to expose a smuggling ring. I saw his wife, a junior constable in the Rajasthan Police, who, together with Dinesh, adopted an orphan girl and took her out of the clutches of people who would have sold her. I saw an old librarian worried about his tenant so much that he asked the police for help. I saw my assistant, Ashok—a man who usually tries to keep out of trouble and controversies—throw caution to the wind and dive right into an armed compound at the sight of captive children. I was also surprised by a colleague whom I had never met before, leading a daring raid against a gang on my word alone. Lastly, I saw a wonderful reporter relentlessly hunting down answers, knowing full well that it may cost her job," Shankar said and stopped.

Nitya smiled. "Well said, Shankar. But you missed one thing."

"What?"

"A handsome police officer who defied orders to uncover what happened to Dinesh. And, of course, to save those poor souls and return Aria to her mother," Nitya added.

"Well, it wasn't all me. The local police were involved; of course, there were Ashok and Anjali."

"I know, but that's not what I meant. Sure, others were

involved in the operation, but you led the investigation that busted the ring. And let's not forget, you risked being ostracised by your peers to find out who from your department may have been involved," Nitya added.

"Hmm." Shankar turned to gaze out the large window.

"Shankar?"

"Yes," he said, quickly turning his gaze back to Nitya.

"What is it?"

Shankar sighed, locked eyes with her, and smiled. But it was a sad smile. "Initially, they were happy with the outcome. But I think I rattled the cage too much. It didn't go down well with higher-ups in the ministry, learning that my superiors at the station were unaware of corrupt personnel in their midst. That started a lot of finger-pointing. Ultimately, they decided the best thing would be to transfer the officer who'd stirred the pot."

"What? That makes no sense. You should have been given a commendation, even a medal, for what you did," Nitya scoffed.

"Oh, I did. I got all sorts of compliments, a special award from the ministry, a medal from the department, and then, when all the dust settled, a transfer order out of the station—and this city," Shankar said, his voice low. He reached for his cup and took a sip.

"Oh! Where are you going?"

"Goa, in a couple of weeks. I have been ordered to join the station in Panaji," Shankar said.

Nitya studied his reaction. Although Goa was a beautiful place, she knew that the posting was a climb down from the high-profile cases Shankar handled in Delhi. As the news sank in, she suddenly realised how much she would miss him. He just sat there, staring at his tea before averting his gaze toward the restaurant entrance. She tried to cheer him up.

"Goa has wonderful beaches, and who knows? You might finally get to relax and have fun," Nitya said, trying to keep her tone chipper.

Shankar smiled. "True. Of all the places I could have ended up, Goa isn't bad."

"You may have some free time to do other things."

"I don't know. I have always been a policeman before anything. You are right, though. Maybe I will take up a hobby, something I have never done before."

"Perhaps sailing or boating? Snorkelling?"

Shankar laughed. "Perhaps. I will tell you what I am looking forward to, though."

"What?"

"I have asked Vikram and Rohini to join me during Vikram's summer vacation."

"Oh!" Nitya blurted, averting her gaze. Her heart sank at his words, and she hesitated before asking, "Does this mean you and Rohini will be getting back together?"

"Oh, I don't know about that," Shankar said, slumping into his chair. "One step at a time. I mean, Goa has good schools, and Vikram could start there. And Rohini is a teacher. Maybe she could look at doing something there, but ..."

"But what?"

"They are well settled in Mussoorie. Vikram has finally adjusted to his school, and Rohini is a teacher there. Plus, she wanted to be close to her parents. I think we will start with this summer vacation and go from there," Shankar said thoughtfully.

Nitya swallowed hard. "But you want them to be with you, right?"

"For Vikram's sake, yes. The good thing about living in Delhi was that I could visit Dehradun on short notice, even on the weekends. I won't be able to do that from Goa. I don't know. Sometimes, I feel Rohini and I owe it to Vikram to give it another go, but then I see her so happy where she is. I am not sure," Shankar said, shaking his head.

"Well, I'm certain you will figure it out. And Goa will be different. It's more laid back compared to Delhi. Besides, Vikram's older now, and if Rohini is working, not staying at home and fretting about you all the time, it may be different," Nitya said.

"We will see. Rohini and I don't talk much anymore. I suspect she thinks the problem isn't exactly the place, whether it be Delhi or Goa, but me," Shankar declared.

Nitya shot him a playful smile. "I think you may be overthinking this."

"Perhaps. Well, we will see how things go. For now, I am just happy that I will get to see Vikram during his vacation."

"That's grand," Nitya said. Before she could say more, the waiter came to refill their cups. They paused to sip their fresh tea, and Nitya turned to gaze at the park, where some elderly couples were strolling across the grass, holding hands.

"I took your advice, by the way," Shankar said.

"About what?" Nitya asked.

"I took some time and found out why I was feeling so tired and exhausted all the time," Shankar responded.

"And?"

"Nothing earth-shattering. Just a lack of sleep and stress," Shankar said. "I mean, I knew that already. But the doctor told me that the recurring dream was because of psychological stress."

"What dream?" Nitya asked. She then gave Shankar her undivided attention as he recounted his surreal trip to the clock store and the strange encounter with the store owner, who resembled an older version of himself.

"What do you think?" Shankar asked once he finished. The question caught Nitya off guard.

"Wow! I don't know what to say. I am surprised you remember your dream in such great detail. Most people forget upon waking," Nitya noted.

"You are right." Shankar nodded. "But the good thing is, I don't have them anymore. The dream seems to have simply vanished."

"How did the doctor explain that?"

"His theory was that my transfer to Goa and my upcoming visit from Vikram have something to do with it. I am more relaxed and looking to the future. Or something along those lines," Shankar said.

Nitya narrowed her eyes. "You don't seem convinced."

"We will see," Shankar said.

"I am sure you have your theory. I am all ears if you want to share," Nitya continued.

Shankar grinned before responding. "You are probably the only person I can think of to share it with."

"And?"

A few seconds ticked by. Finally, Shankar muttered, "Loneliness."

"You think you are lonely, and that's what triggered the dream?"

Shankar shrugged. "I don't know."

"You have been on your own before," Nitya suggested.

"Yes, but there is a difference between being alone and being lonely," Shankar reasoned with a sad smile.

"True," Nitya agreed. "Maybe Goa will help. I hope it does, for your sake."

"Well, enough about me," Shankar said, wiping his hands on

his napkin. "What did you want to tell me or ask me?" Shankar slowly took another sip.

Nitya tilted her head, feigning confusion. She knew exactly what he was referring to, but she needed time. "What?" she asked.

"When I arrived earlier, you said you had to tell me something," Shankar continued.

Nitya waved it off. "Oh, it's just what we talked about. Being let go from my job, the new opportunity with the London paper," she said quickly.

"Nothing else?" Shankar pressed, furrowing his brow.

Nitya hesitated before adding, "No, nothing else." She looked away, hoping he'd let it go. When she turned back to him, she found Shankar smiling at her.

"You know, Nitya, I am a police officer," he said slowly.

Nitya laughed. "Don't I know it? And a very good one, may I add," she said, nodding.

Shankar's grin widened. "Good enough to know that something's on my friend's mind, and she doesn't want to share it with me."

Nitya shook her head as Shankar leaned forward. "Nothing to add, Shankar." She forced a smile.

"All right, I won't press you. But if you ever want to talk, and you feel it is the right moment, please call me any time," Shankar said.

"I will. You are the only person I can talk to about everything," Nitya said. After a brief pause, the waiter arrived with the bill, and despite Shankar's fervent protests, Nitya took care of it. They exited the restaurant and meandered to the gardens, where they found a bench next to an ice cream cart.

"Ice cream?" Shankar asked.

Nitya chuckled. "Always!"

Shankar got up, and Nitya watched as he strode to the vendor to order two orange cream bars. Nitya closed her eyes and tilted her face to the bright sky, letting her mind wander. A gentle nudge on her shoulder drew her back to the present. She opened her eyes to see Shankar standing before her, ice cream in hand.

"Lost in London, are we?" Shankar asked.

Nitya smiled warmly, thanked him, and quickly took the orange bar. They sat side by side on the bench, devouring their cold treat as they watched people enjoying the mild weather and going about their lives.

Acknowledgements

Writing is a solitary endeavour, but that doesn't mean authors exist in isolation. Since I started my literary journey nearly five years ago, there have been so many people who have encouraged me. Chief among them is my family – my wife and daughters who have been fascinated with the stories and my odyssey – the sense of adventure, doing something new and different, the accolades that have come with it, and above all, the enjoyment I have derived from it. My parents have always been a constant in my life and my mother, who normally doesn't read English fiction, has endured and enjoyed all my books.

The one regret I do have is that the one person who would have really gotten a kick out of my novels and been the proudest, my father, didn't get to see any of my published works. He passed away a few months before my first book – if one believes in providence and cosmic miracles, then I suppose he has a smile on his face wherever he is. My father was and remains the best storyteller I ever knew.

Secret of the Missing Tenant is my first collaboration with the incredibly talented Suhail Mathur, my literary agent, who spearheads one of India's foremost literary agencies, The Book Bakers. Suhail has been instrumental in representing this book and I am grateful to him and The Book Bakers for their guidance and championing my work. I hope this is the start of a fruitful partnership. I want to thank Arup Bose and his excellent team at

Srishti Publishers & Distributors for believing in the story and for all their efforts in making it successful.

I also want to extend my gratitude and thanks to Brooke De Lira – for her help throughout the writing and editing process – her feedback, revisions, and suggestions to make the book better. Brooke has been a part of many of my books – an association that has been both wonderful and enjoyable.